Tiger!

Tiger!

GEOFFREY MALONE

Hodder
Children's
Books

a division of Hodder Headline Limited

A Catalogue record for this book is available from
the British Library

ISBN-10: 0 340 89358 3
ISBN-13: 978 0 340 89358 6

Typeset in Baskerville by Avon DataSet Ltd,
Bidford on Avon, Warwickshire

Printed and bound in Great Britain by
Bookmarque Ltd, Croydon, Surrey

The paper and board used in this paperback by Hodder Children's Books
are natural recyclable products made from wood grown in sustainable
forests. The manufacturing processes conform to the environmental
regulations of the country of origin.

Hodder Children's Books
a division of Hodder Headline Limited
338 Euston Road
London NW1 3BH

To Krid and Pui Panyarachun
With love

1

Kuma froze. One great paw held motionless, a centimetre above the ground. She stared straight ahead. All her senses concentrated on the tree fifty metres in front of her. And on the sambar stag feeding beside it, black and tempting in the misty, pre-dawn light.

It was an old stag with a ruff of long hair around its neck and years of successful survival behind it. Kuma held her breath as the animal looked up and turned its head towards her. She saw the ears twitch and the mouth abruptly stop its chewing. The antlers tossed and the stag pawed the ground. The sound of its hooves carried across the hard-packed earth that lay between them. The hair along Kuma's spine stiffened.

She knew the antelope was uneasy. Some deep-seated instinct had alerted it, but what that was, Kuma could not tell. Some tiny worry or uncertainty had warned the sambar to look up at that precise moment. It might just be an unseen swirl of air brushing the leaves above its head. There were no other animals moving out here and certainly not the langur monkeys who infested these trees in the daylight. They were the eyes and ears of the forest and had they been awake, their warning screams would long ago have panicked the deer.

Besides, Kuma was certain the sambar had not seen or heard her careful approach through the elephant grass. But sambars were not easy prey to catch. They were shy animals and swift runners. Much faster than a tiger. They could detect the slightest rustle and spot the smallest suspicious movement, like a stalk of grass shivering on a still morning. A tiger had to get very close to have any chance of pulling one down.

So Kuma waited, sensing that the stag was not yet sufficiently alarmed to turn tail and make a bolt for it. If that happened, there would be no point in the tigress giving chase. To have any chance of catching the stag, Kuma needed to get within at least thirty metres of it, before launching her attack.

She had hardly eaten for the past eight days. Only carrion: three dead crows and a mongoose she had found deep in the forest, where the vultures couldn't fly. But in the last forty-eight hours she had eaten nothing at all so that now her skin hung loose and empty along her sides. So she waited, her body rigid with anticipation, willing the deer to turn its head and resume grazing. Only the tip of her tail, flicking from side to side, betrayed her intense excitement. And her desperation.

For the first time in her life, Kuma's skills as a hunter seemed to have deserted her. Days and nights of patient stalking and frantic chases had brought her nothing. Just the increasing fear of failure, as a procession of terrified blackbuck and chitals dodged and feinted and somehow wrong-footed her. Every final leap only brought her a mouthful of dust. At first, she had stared after each escaping antelope in disbelief. But for the last two days, a strange new fear was beginning to sap her confidence. Each failed attack was draining away just a little bit more of her stamina. Her attacks were becoming shorter and shorter as her energy flagged. And all the time, the cubs inside her kicked with growing urgency.

In the trees behind Kuma, a red jungle cock began to crow. It was answered by the piercing cry of a peafowl. The forest was awakening. Other birds were sleepily joining in the chorus. A jackal was barking. Soon the sun would rise like a huge copper ball, flooding the forest and the dusty plains beyond with brilliant light. In an hour's time, the heat would lie like an iron bar across the backs of every waking creature. The sambar looked high over Kuma's head towards the dawn and shook itself, suddenly reassured.

The sambar was moving now. Turning away from the tigress with its back towards her. As Kuma watched, the stag stood on its hind legs and stared up at the tree. It reached for a high branch where the leaves were more tender and began tugging at them.

Kuma's eyes narrowed. She saw a stag with

massive antlers, almost two metres high at the shoulder. Two hundred kilos of meat. A rush of saliva filled her mouth. She must eat. She had to. Without meat, there would be no milk for her cubs. No hope of their surviving. Then she was coming forward, her stomach brushing the ground, slipping through the high grass like a shadow, following the sound of rustling branches. A tawny ghost. Unseen, unexpected and merciless.

She stopped and raised her head, taking great care not to be seen. Twenty metres from the tree, the grass became patchy, giving way to large tussocks scattered at random across the red earth. In front of her, the sambar stood, neck extended, nibbling at a hanging branch. She heard the clatter of hooves on the trunk as it almost overbalanced.

At the edge of the grass, Kuma sank to the ground. The sambar's scent filled her nostrils and her mouth watered uncontrollably. Her body shook. She felt weak with anticipation. She crawled forward a few more centimetres. Then slowly, with infinite care, she gathered herself to spring. As she took the final breath, a bird screamed a warning from a bush somewhere to her right.

In one flowing movement, the sambar looked around, leapt down and was off, racing for its life, hooves kicking up small puffs of dust. It took Kuma a split second to react. In that time, the stag had gained another four metres on her. Then she too was racing in pursuit, all her pent-up frustration driving her on in great leaping bounds.

The stag was a good thirty metres in front, almost out of range. Kuma never took her eyes off the animal's rump, watching for any sudden flexing of muscle that would signal a change in direction. A blood lust drove her on. It was an adrenalin rush of confidence, far stronger than anything she had ever felt before.

She was gaining on the stag, silently powering over the ground in long, easy, ten-metre strides, shrinking the distance between them. The sambar sensed this and panicked. It began a long curving run towards the line of forest, a kilometre away. Kuma cut across to intercept. They were less than twenty metres apart now and white froth was gathering along the stag's mouth.

Then they were weaving in and out of a jumble of termite hills. The ground was broken and rutted. The sambar slipped and its shoulder thudded into the side of an ant-hill. As it fought to stay upright, a snake's head darted out of a nearby hole. For a fraction of a second their eyes met then the sambar was past. But in that brief moment, the stag had forgotten where the tiger had been. Its eyes bulged. The sambar jinked to the left, dodged through a gap between two high mounds and ran straight into Kuma's path.

The tigress sprang, claws extended, digging deep into the packed muscle of the animal's rump. The sambar screamed and leapt vertically, trying to throw the tiger off. But Kuma's claws were too long and her need too great. The next instant she battered her great weight down on to the stag's back, forcing it to its knees in a terrible, bone-cracking slide.

Before the stag could do anything, Kuma flung a massive forepaw around its neck, swung her weight like a pivot and heaved the animal over on to its side. As they slid across the ground, she sank her teeth into its neck, biting down into the jugular.

Hot blood spurted into the tiger's mouth. The taste of it almost made Kuma loosen her grip. She was dizzy with elation and her eyes closed in pure relief. The blood ran down her chest and gathered in a dark stain under her body.

But the sambar was still struggling. Kicking out frantically with its razor-edged hooves. One lucky blow would break the tiger's leg and sentence Kuma herself to death from starvation. The stag was making a huge effort to hoist itself back on to its feet. Kuma's jaws clamped over its muzzle, cutting off the oxygen supply. She forced the animal's head back and pinned it to the ground with a paw. The sambar's struggles weakened. It gave a last violent shudder and lay still. When she was satisfied that the deer was dead, Kuma let go and slumped down alongside it, too exhausted even to eat.

2

Kuma slept for almost half an hour before the sound of squabbling woke her. She lay on her side and watched the vultures work themselves into a frenzy. They hissed and gobbled at her to get on with the feast. There must have been a hundred of them, the bravest within a few metres of the tigress.

She sat up and looked around. There were more vultures watching from the tops of the termite hills. Every so often, one of them would fly down into the middle of the crowd. They landed with beating wings and tried to force their way through to the front. Kuma made no effort to move. She was enjoying the feel of the sun on her face. Then one of the birds came too close. With a snarl, Kuma rolled over on to her feet and stood over the body.

The vultures shrank back. Kuma saw that the sambar's eyes were already glazed. She licked the body and the taste made her drool. She stalked round to the rear of the stag and squatted down on her elbows, like some huge domestic tabby. She began to drag off the skin with powerful rasps of her tongue. The vultures screamed and beat at each other in excitement. Like all tigers, Kuma always began to eat here. A leopard would have slashed open the stomach and dragged out the liver. A wild dog pack would already have devoured everything.

She ate steadily all the way through the morning, until the sun was high overhead. By then, she was gorged and the skin over her stomach was stretched like a drum. She had eaten almost twenty kilograms of meat and could not take a mouthful more. She rolled over on to her back and lay with all four legs in the air. She squinted up into the bleached sky and saw a black spiral of crows circling there. They were also watching her, willing her to finish. She knew too, that every predator for miles would have seen them and would know what their presence meant.

Kuma considered. There was enough meat left on the kill for several more days. But out here, there was nowhere to hide the carcass. She was strong enough to drag it back to the forest but if she did that, she knew it would hasten the birth. And to have cubs out here in the open was unthinkable. The sky was also full of predators. They would swoop and seize the cubs the moment her back was turned. Besides, she had already found a secret place to give birth. But she was still reluctant to surrender the sambar to the scavengers. If she did, there would be nothing left of it in half an hour. Only the skull, the hooves and a few splintered bones would be left. It was a problem she had never had to face before.

In the end, it was thirst that decided her. It was the hot season when the sun seemed to suck every bit of moisture out of every living creature. By midday it was so hot that even the snakes lay in loose coils, panting at the bottom of the termite mounds. It was time to head back to the stream that ran through her territory. Time to spend the rest of the afternoon cooling off. It was time to go.

She smelt the carcass a couple more times then deliberately squatted and marked it. The vultures rose in a ragged wave as she left. A pair of hyenas watched her coming and sidled out of her way. Kuma looked over her shoulder. The kill had already disappeared under the crush of birds. She thought about charging them or even taking back the kill, but her mouth was too dry.

She plodded across the plain, her head down and her long pink tongue hanging slack. A swarm of flies hung around her head, attracted by the smell of blood. Their bodies gleamed blue and green. She walked for a kilometre before entering the shade of the forest. She made no pretence at concealment and at once an angry babble of noise erupted. High overhead, langur monkeys peered down and spat at her. They followed her, running along the branches and swinging from tree to tree, screaming a warning to every other forest dweller.

A flock of parrots exploded out of the bushes in a flurry of red and gold and flew through the treetops, protesting shrilly to one another. Herds of chitals and blackbuck stood nervously in the forest clearings and watched her go by, their tails flickering with uncertainty.

At last, Kuma reached the stream. She slid down the bank and lay full length in the shallows. She drank with her chin resting on the gravel bottom. When she could drink no more, she put her face under the surface and let the water wash the dust out of her eyes and nostrils. Then she lay still, listening to the sound of insects overhead.

A shoal of tiny fish was nibbling at the hair on her paws. Intrigued, she followed their darting movements. Then it dawned on her. They were feeding on the sambar's blood. Carefully, she lifted the other paw clear of the stream, waited, and brought it down with a smack. When the water cleared, there was no sign of them.

She yawned and closed her eyes. The next moment, a sharp, stabbing pain gripped her insides. She yelped in shock and knew immediately what was happening. As she struggled up, the contraction began to fade. But she was already climbing out of the stream.

She walked with increasing urgency back into

the forest and up a tangled hillside. A family of wild pig blundered out of the undergrowth and began rooting around in front of her. Kuma waited in the shadows, willing them to go. When they realised she was there, they stood petrified with fear then barged into each other, struggling to get past. The old boar swung round, his tusks gleaming, and bravely challenged her while his family ran for their lives. Kuma snarled at him. The contractions were starting again and she wanted him out of the way. He held his ground until she roared at him in rage. He jumped back in shock and bolted.

She reached the tumble of massive boulders near the top of the hill and stood listening. Way below her, the wild pigs crashed through the undergrowth. Eventually, the squealings died away and the forest was quiet again. She looked back down the way she had come, but nothing caught her eye. She was not being followed. Up here, only the butterflies moved. She paced up and down, searching for signs of any other animals, especially predators like leopards, who would eagerly devour a tiger cub. But she found nothing. There were no suspicious scents or pugmarks anywhere.

She walked towards a long vertical crack in the rocks that looked far too narrow to squeeze through. At its base, thick, overhanging ferns concealed a narrow entrance that gave no indication of the cave inside. With a final look around, she bent and pushed her way through. She waited until her eyes grew used to the darkness.

She lay down on the dry, sandy floor and carefully rolled over on to her side, listening to the world outside. The hum of insects and wild bees and the occasional call of a bird. Satisfied, she closed her eyes, and began to moan.

3

Kuma's cubs were born in the late afternoon. There were three of them and a sad little bundle of fur that lay silent and unmoving on the floor of the cave. Kuma stooped and carried it to the far side, well away from the entrance. Later, she would eat it. A stream of blowflies or wasps flying in and out of the cave could mean only one thing to a passing predator.

She went back to her kittens and stood staring down in fascination. Three tiny replicas of herself squirmed and mewed and fell over one another as they searched blindly for their mother and her milk. Three perfect little tigers, fully striped across their heads and backs with fluffy white undersides.

Bewildered little creatures with wobbly legs and outsize paws, weighing not much more than a bag of sugar, and utterly helpless. It would be a week at least before their eyes opened. She had never seen anything so wonderful. Kuma marvelled at them and felt an intense wave of love engulf her.

She lay down facing them. For the next two years, until they left her, they would be her obsession. Everything she did would be done to protect them and equip them to survive to adulthood. But only one of the cubs was ever likely to get that far, despite her ferocious love. Forest fires, floods, disease or even snakebite would all take their toll.

Kuma put her head on her paws and watched the way they wrinkled their noses and butted each other. She reached out and cradled them to her with her paw. They were ridiculously small, a tiny fraction of her own size. A great maternal pride seized her and it was time for her to start being a proper mother to them.

She held each cub in turn between her paws and washed it with her long, pink tongue. A tongue strong enough to rasp the hide off an antelope's back now gently cleared the blood from miniature nostrils and ears. The cubs struggled to break free, yowling in protest. They were even more furious when she rolled them on to their backs and cleaned their undersides. They hissed at her and raked at her chin with their ridiculously large feet.

She rubbed her cheek along their bodies, marvelling at their perfection. She loved their warmth and the sound of their hearts pulsing with life. She sensed their determination to do what they wanted, which right now, was to feed. She called to them for the very first time and saw them respond immediately. Despite their blindness, they found her and the places to feed. Soon all three cubs were nuzzling her, their heads pressing into her side, suckling contentedly.

For the first time in her life, Kuma began to purr. She was happy. In all her four years, she had never experienced anything like this before. It was a feeling of pure pleasure. She closed her eyes to enjoy it all the more. In the past, only eating had made her happy. That, and no longer having her stomach ache with hunger. But never, ever, had there been anything like this. And certainly not during her mating with Raji.

Raji was a newcomer who had fought and driven off her own father. Six months ago, he had appeared from nowhere, challenging to take over the territory and become the dominant male. This territory included Kuma's home range, all of her mother's and an older half-sister's. Together, the three females occupied almost forty square kilometres of dry forest and open plain. It was good territory, with enough deer and other prey to support them all. Each tigress needed at least one large meal a week and the territory provided that. Finding and killing that prey was then up to them.

There was no shortage of water. The same stream ran through all their ranges. It was fed by a spring high up in the surrounding hills. It never ran dry even in the hottest weather. To the tigers, it was their most precious resource. Unlike lions who enjoyed lying out on the sun-baked plains, tigers needed shade. Kuma and the others would spend hours in the water, keeping cool during the heat of the day.

And so, Raji had challenged for all this and the mating rights that went with it. At six years old, he was in his prime, weighing close to three hundred kilograms and over three metres long. He was twice the size of Kuma. She knew he would win the very first time she heard him roar. He was so full of confidence.

The whole forest listened in silence as the two males battled it out. They met in a clearing, their eyes bright with hate. They circled each other, watching and assessing, walking stiffly with their claws fully extended. They fought chest to chest, their bodies thudding together with a force that could be felt a hundred metres away. They reared up on their hind legs, jaws wide open, dagger-like teeth striking at the other's neck.

Kuma crouched with her belly pressed to the ground, listening wide-eyed to the spittings and screams until at last she heard her father's long, agonised howl. It was the beginning of the end. Then the rain had come beating down, muffling Raji's triumphant roars.

Kuma and Raji mated two months later. For three days they stayed together, mating frequently.

There was little joy in it for Kuma and much resentment on her part at this male intrusion. When it was finally over, she spun around and raked him with her claws. He left her with blood streaming from deep scratches across his nose. But now she was glad that he was the father of her cubs. They would have his protection while they were growing up.

Later, when Kuma woke, the cubs were still asleep. They lay in a small heap, their heads close to her side. Carefully, she eased herself upright and stretched. It brought the blood racing back through cramped muscles. She grimaced in pain. She was thirsty and remembered the stream. She licked her lips and pushed the thought from her mind. She would only leave the cubs when she was desperate to drink.

She bent over them and listened to their steady breathing. Reassured, she padded over to the entrance and stood behind the screen of ferns. Outside, the day was coming to an end. A faint breeze was starting up as cooler air flowed across the baking rocks. In half an hour, it would be dark and the night would be filling with new sounds and cries. Night was the time when most of the killing was done.

She listened intently for the smallest sign of danger. And she knew what form it would probably take. Leopards. They were her greatest fear and hilltops were places they favoured. They used rocky outcrops like this to stare down into the forest in search of prey. Finding a safe den was not easy. She had to choose between the high rocks, and risk leopards, or staying on the forest floor where other killers waited. Predators such as hyenas and jackals, sloth bears too. And the most ruthless of all, the wild dog packs.

She had spent many hours examining these rocks. She had waited here at night and in the daytime to see if any leopards came. But she had found nothing. There were no old scent marks on the tumbling undergrowth. No pugmarks between the great boulders and no sign at all of long claw slashes down the sides of trees.

The place seemed clear of them but despite this she remained watchful. Leopards were cunning animals. Far more so than tigers. And the two species hated each other. The cubs were going to be especially vulnerable for the next year. Even after that, they would only have their milk teeth to protect them and would be no match for a determined leopard.

Towards dawn, when she had fed the cubs for a third time, Kuma slipped outside and sat upright on a boulder like a huge cat. It felt good to be in the open again. By human reckoning, the night was pitch dark. A layer of cloud was blotting out the starlight, a warning of the approaching monsoon. She had no difficulty seeing – her night-sight was excellent – and her hearing was equally sharp.

She heard a faint rattling noise some distance below and cocked her head to listen. The sound was unmistakable. A porcupine was busy searching for food. Hurrying along, with its nose pressed close to the ground, its long, thin outer quills bending and tapping against the thicker ones underneath. Every forest animal knew the sound and, if they were wise, kept out of its way.

Porcupines were delicious to eat but almost certain death to the inexperienced hunter. Their quills were as sharp as needles and designed to break off deep inside an attacker's body. Death almost always followed either from blood-poisoning or slow starvation. She remembered finding a young male tiger, lying on its side, too weak too move. It was almost a skeleton with its hip bones poking through the skin. But it was the paws Kuma remembered best.

They were swollen to twice their normal size and oozing pus. Quills, the size of old bamboo shoots, had broken off deep inside the pads of both front paws. There were more of them in the shoulder and legs. There were teeth marks in both paws and patches of raw skin on the shins, where the tiger had tried to pull them out. But the remnants had remained embedded.

The very next night, she had met a porcupine herself. She was about five metres from a fallen tree when she heard the sudden rattle of quills. She snarled at the animal and crouched. As she did so, the porcupine bristled and the very next moment began to run backwards towards her. If she had not seen the dead tiger for herself, she would have attacked it. Instead, she just had time to leap to one side. As the porcupine rushed past, she hit it on the side of the head and killed it stone-dead.

Cautiously, she flipped it over on to its back and began to tear at the exposed underbelly. But Kuma had learnt a lesson and would pass that information on to her cubs, when the time was right.

She listened now to the sound of digging and sheets of earth spraying out on all sides. The porcupine was grunting with the effort. Kuma guessed it was tugging at a root. Moments later, it began to eat. When it finished, it shook itself with a loud rattle and hurried on its way.

She swished her tail angrily and leapt down. Inside the cave, the cubs had not moved. She yawned and lay down with them. A minute later she was fast asleep.

4

Inspector Singh was staring critically at a large wooden board. It was nailed to the wall outside his office. The board was painted red and had white lettering. The words, 'Indian Wildlife Service . . . Kanla National Tiger Park . . . Park Headquarters,' ran across the lower half of the board in three unsteady rows. Someone had made a brave attempt to reproduce a snarling tiger above it.

Inspector Singh frowned. Then he stood back and shook his head. 'It's no good, Ambrose. It needs redoing,' he said.

'. . . needs redoing . . .' the man beside him murmured, writing busily. He was holding a large notebook.

'The letters are all different sizes,' the Inspector complained. 'Look! Here! And there! They're all over the place. And that tiger looks as if it's got really bad breath. This is useless! We need a proper sign-writer.'

'. . . different sizes . . .' the other echoed.

Inspector Singh turned and studied a smaller sign on the other side of his door. It read, 'Inspector D.B. Singh . . . Temporary Park Commander'.

'Temporary!' He snorted. 'Temporary! I've been here, man and boy, for the past twenty years. There's nothing "Temporary" about me! Is there, Ambrose?'

The other shook his head. 'No, Inspector! Certainly not. Very permanent.'

Inspector Singh smiled at this witticism. He was a stocky man with a weather-beaten face and laughter lines at the corners of his eyes and mouth. There were two silver stars on each shoulder of his starched khaki shirt. The sleeves were rolled back above his elbows revealing strong forearms covered with black hair.

'You're going to have to take it into town,

Ambrose, and get it done properly. This is hopeless.'

Ambrose cleared his throat. He was a tall, thin man with a pronounced stoop. He was the chief clerk at the headquarters and looked after the day-to-day administration of the Park. 'It won't be cheap,' he warned. 'It'll probably cost a lot. People in Amra think we've got money to burn.'

'Money!' thought Inspector Singh. 'The never-ending problem of money. Or rather, the lack of it.' It often kept him awake at nights. He saw Ambrose shaking his head and shrugged. It had to be done. The Park would have to pay for it. There was no other choice.

A sign-writer in the local town would charge an arm and a leg for doing it. Everyone charged exorbitant rates for anything to do with the Park. It was their way of getting their own back. It was the same all over India. Wherever there were parks or animal reserves like Kanla, there was resentment from the local people.

The truth was there were just too many human beings and they all needed land to support themselves on. And around here, Inspector Singh reflected, almost all of them thought it was terrible that the two hundred square miles the Park occupied were reserved exclusively for animals.

Every year, more and more people entered the Park illegally. They burnt the jungle and cleared the ground for planting crops. Some of their smallholdings were not found for months and by that time, it was too late. The damage was already done. The herds of blackbuck and chitals would quickly move away, taking the tigers with them. The more human beings encroached, the less natural habitat was left for wildlife. It was a vicious circle. Then, there was the ever present threat of poachers, but Inspector Singh thrust that thought away from him.

Officially, no one was allowed to farm or graze cattle inside the Park. Nor could they gather firewood or take clean water from the streams and ponds. Many people did, of course, and sometimes a tiger killed one of them. That only made matters worse. Every time it happened, the newspaper in Amra, the nearest town, worked itself up into a froth of indignation. For years, its editorial line had been that tigers were treated better than people. The paper played a leading part in fanning the flames of local resentment.

Ambrose was talking to him. 'I can go into Amra this afternoon,' he was saying, 'and see who I can find. He'll want a cash advance, of course. A thousand rupees at least. I'll need to take it with me.'

'Money, money, money!' Inspector Singh glared at Ambrose then shook his head. 'This is the fourth biggest tiger sanctuary in India and we run it on a shoestring! We can't even afford to give the offices a lick of paint.'

'Or have the roof properly repaired,' grumbled Ambrose. 'I'm dreading the next monsoon.'

'You'd better tell your clerks to buy a big umbrella each,' Inspector Singh snorted. He waved a hand at the buildings grouped around the Headquarters. 'The British built this place a hundred years ago,' he said. 'As a veterinary hospital for their army horses and mules. The only thing we've done since they left is add on the elephant stables.' He shook his head. 'OK! Let's get on with things.'

Inspector Singh was carrying out his regular

weekly inspection. Ambrose followed him as he went through every room in the headquarters. Inspector Singh strode past desks and filing cabinets and talked to each of the clerks working there.

The next stop was the cookhouse. Inspector Singh did not like the senior cook. 'He's on the fiddle,' he grunted to Ambrose at the door.

Ambrose blinked in surprise. 'Of course he is. You always say that.'

Inspector Singh checked the battered pans and cooking trays for cleanliness. He prodded a sack of onions and discovered several of the bottom layers were bad. He looked behind a lavatory door and found a half-eaten chicken leg, black with ants. The senior cook made a rude gesture at his retreating back.

'We'll do the stores, next!' Inspector Singh told Ambrose. 'Then take a look at the elephants, if you can walk that far.' He grinned. The run-in with the cook had restored his good humour.

Ambrose looked at his watch. 'And it's time for a cup of tea. Joshi will have one brewing for us.'

'Best cuppa in India,' Inspector Singh agreed. 'I

don't know what he puts into it but I wish my wife would do the same.'

Ambrose was amused. 'I don't think Mrs Singh would be too pleased to hear you say that.'

Inspector Singh laughed. 'She'd have my guts for garters. And I'll have yours, if you ever tell her!'

Ambrose smiled. 'How are Anji and Himal liking their school?'

Inspector Singh considered. 'It's all a bit new for Anji of course, but she seems to be making friends. Himal still doesn't like getting up so early but he did well enough last term. Frankly, so long as they've got the elephants to help with at the weekends, they're happy.'

They walked the next hundred metres in a companionable silence. Then, 'See that bush?' Inspector Singh said, pointing. 'A spitting cobra fell out of it two years ago, right in front of me. If I'd have been a metre closer it would have got me.'

'I saw a dog once that had been attacked,' Ambrose reminisced. 'Its head was swollen twice the size and all the skin had peeled off.'

'Nice things snakes,' said Inspector Singh drily. 'Baby elephants are fascinated by them. One or two get bitten every year and die.' He turned to Ambrose. 'Remind me, will you, to check the anti-venom stocks when we get to the medical centre.'

5

Kuma was hunting. All her senses tuned to the never-ending search for food. She leapt silently down into a gully and followed it along. Down here, she was screened from view, making it easier to spot a potential prey against the growing dawn. She moved silently, her paws stirring up a curtain of fine dust that hung in the air for several minutes.

Overhead, an owl flew back to its tree. Kuma watched it fold its wings and land on a jagged branch. She heard it complaining to itself. Like her, it had not had a successful night's hunting. She saw a large stand of bamboo not far ahead. Smaller animals might be hiding there. Perhaps even a mongoose searching for snakes. It was worth a try.

She circled the bamboo but found nothing. Frustrated and hungry, she sat down and scratched. Then she started worrying about the cubs. Should she go back and check on them? The cubs were nine months old and the size and weight of large dogs. They had left the cave six months ago and by now were used to following Kuma from kill to kill. But they were still utterly dependent on her. Until their own canine teeth came through in another year's time, they could not kill for themselves. Their milk teeth were quite unable to pierce the tough hide of an antelope.

Kuma hesitated, unsure what to do. She had hunted all night and still had nothing to show for it. She was very hungry and knew the cubs would be too. Should she leave them for a little longer or go back to them? The previous evening, she had settled the cubs in tall grass close to some wild plum bushes. Even though she knew they would stay out of sight, there was always the worry that something unexpected might have happened.

Then she saw the elephant tracks and stopped. She looked around warily, glad now that the cubs were not with her. She bent and examined the tracks. They were fresh. The sun had not yet sucked the dew out of the dust, so that the sides of each footprint stood out sharp and well defined. There were no ant or insect trails running across the bottom of the footmarks. Or any wind-blown seeds or pieces of grass lying there. This elephant had gone past less than twenty minutes ago. It might even be watching her now.

Kuma looked up, a growl thickening in her throat. She looked over both shoulders. There was danger here. Elephants could move as quietly as any tiger. And they could run, surprisingly quickly. The two species hated each other and a careless tiger made an irresistible target. One blow from a trunk would smash her ribs and leave her to be bayoneted at leisure. Or stamped underfoot. She walked on with her tail held out stiffly behind and her eyes very wide.

And then, faintly, she heard the sound of splashing. It was unmistakable. It grew louder. She tried to ignore it but after a while, her curiosity got the better of her. She stopped to listen, unable to decide if it was just one animal or several making the noise. She remembered the large watering-hole and knew it was coming from there. She turned towards the sound and went forward.

She took care to keep in cover. There were not many tall trees in this part of the forest and hardly any monkeys. But there were always crows and peacocks ready to warn others of her presence. Somewhere too, there was an elephant. No one, however, saw her creep forward to the line of bushes that screened the water hole. She sank down on her haunches and very cautiously edged forward.

A wild pig stood up to its middle in the water with a length of purple waterweed hanging from its mouth. It was surrounded by lily pads. Behind it, there was a dense patch of bulrushes. Without a moment's hesitation, Kuma raced down a long sandy bank towards it. The pig saw her coming and gave a high-pitched squeal. It turned and began floundering towards the rushes, forcing its way through the water. It looked back, panicked and went under with a loud splash. Water birds rose in a protesting flock.

There was movement at the corner of Kuma's eye. Instinct made her leap to one side. The boar's head caught her back leg a glancing blow. She winced and spun away, the impact throwing her off balance. She half fell but was on her feet in a flash, panting in shock. The sand was soft and covered her feet.

She could hear frantic splashing and squeals coming from the direction of the water hole but her eyes never left the boar. He stood a metre high and must have weighed close to a hundred and thirty kilograms. Bloodshot eyes set deep above long tusks glared at the tigress. There were scars across his back and shoulders.

Kuma crouched, ears flat against her head. She stole forward and began to circle the boar. She exploded out of the sand with outstretched claws, then leapt aside and twisted away. The boar shook his head and stamped in rage. They circled each other, watching and waiting for an opening. The boar's massive head followed her round, his wicked little eyes glowing.

Kuma rushed in again, spitting and slashing. Blood streamed down the boar's shoulder. Snorting with rage, he turned on her. Kuma sprang to one side. As she landed, she slipped in the loose sand. In a flash, the boar was on her, swinging his tusks down towards her unguarded stomach.

Kuma twisted on to her back and brought all four feet up to cover her belly. She felt her claws ripping through the boar's hide then she was heaving him off her and twisting out from under him. She raced for the cover of the bushes. She heard his hooves pounding after her but knew he would not risk following her in here. She stood panting in deep cover and reconsidered. What had happened to the other pig?

Carefully, Kuma backed out of the thicket, while the boar patrolled up and down, snorting triumphantly. She left him waiting for her to reappear while she made a long, curving detour. After a couple of hundred metres, she stopped to listen. This time, she heard the sound of contented grunting from close at hand.

Moments later, she was looking at the sow, now drinking at the water's edge with its back to her. Kuma killed it with a single bite to the spine. The pig's knees buckled and it died without even a whimper. She carried it in her mouth, a full hundred metres to the edge of the forest. She held her head as far back as she could, to keep the sow's hooves from leaving drag marks in the sand. Her jaws were aching by the time she reached the trees. Kuma took it still deeper into the forest and hid the body in a narrow ravine. She covered it with dead tree branches to hide it from the crows, then, satisfied, she set off at a steady lope. It was time to fetch the cubs.

The cubs were bored and very hungry. They had woken at dawn and for a while stayed motionless, listening to the sounds of the forest. They were cold and stiff and soon huddled close together while the sun's rays turned the sky pink. Taza, the male cub, yawned and slumped against Phur, the larger of the two females. She gave a snarl of protest and swatted him hard on the side of the head.

Delighted, Taza flung himself on her. Phur dodged, then leapt on to his back, biting the back of his neck. Taza wriggled free and they stood locked together, swaying back and forth, biting at each other's jaws.

When they grew bored they groomed themselves. This done, they went to find Poga, the younger female cub. Poga's best friend was a piece of stick. It was her dearest and only possession. She took it everywhere, holding it in her mouth like some enormous cigar. They found her lying on her back rolling it between her paws. Taza pounced and snatched it.

Furious, Poga chased him across the grass towards the plum bushes. Although several kilos lighter, she was the most determined of all the cubs and usually got her own way. She hurled herself at Taza, scratching at his eyes, wanting to hurt. Taza dropped the stick and snarled, suddenly very serious.

Phur watched and waited, then leapt at his head. She hung there, kicking at his chest, before the three of them fell over and rolled across the ground. Poga was the first to worm her way clear. She seized the stick and raced towards the plum bushes where she squeezed herself up into its branches.

The others let her go. Phur lay full length and closed her eyes. Taza cleaned his paws and yawned. The next moment, there was a low cough that brought the cubs sitting up and listening hard. Kuma coughed twice more but by then the cubs were already running to her. They greeted her with yowls of joy and surged in and out of her front legs, rubbing their heads against her chest. Taza lay on his back and kicked at her chin in delight. She licked his paws, then rolled Phur over and buried her head in the cub's fur.

The cubs caught the smell of blood on her and became even more excited. They jostled each other struggling to lick her mouth and tongue. Kuma stopped them with a single, sharp grunt and led them off towards the kill. The cubs trotted after her, Taza leading and Poga, the smallest, bringing up the rear.

When they reached the ravine, Kuma tore the skin away from the pig's rump. Then she bit off chunks of meat and dropped them on the ground. Next, she slashed open the pig's stomach. She gave a low, rolling growl and stood back as the cubs flung themselves on the carcass.

Afterwards, the family lay close together. They spent time grooming each other. Sometimes, the cubs clambered over Kuma, hugging her around the neck and biting her ears. Occasionally, she would grunt in protest and swat them. A little later, she led them to the water hole. There was no sign of the old boar. They sank gratefully into the water and lay there enjoying its coolness. Kuma was still hungry. There had been very little left of the pig. When sunset came, she would start hunting again. But now she was feeling sleepy and the water felt perfect. She closed her eyes and began to doze.

6

At about the same time, a small energetic woman banged a plate of fruit down in front of her son. Then she stood back from the table and rubbed her arms briskly. It was cool out here on the verandah, at this time of the morning. The sun was still below the treetops. It threw long shadows across the patch of withered grass Mrs Singh liked to call 'the lawn'.

'Come on, Himal. Eat up! You're going to be late and you know the school bus won't wait.' Mrs Singh hovered over her son. Her hands made little darting movements, pointing in turn to the rolls of bread and the fruit.

'Why does she always say this to me?' Himal

wondered. Every morning he stayed in bed until he heard his father's moped start up. Then he would leap up and be standing at his window, cleaning his teeth, by the time it puttered past. Ever since he could remember, he had watched his father leave for work at the Park Headquarters, in his crisp, khaki uniform. Just before he turned on to the track that ran past their bungalow, Inspector Singh always waved goodbye then pulled his goggles down over his eyes.

'Your sister's been ready for the last ten minutes.'

Himal scowled and stuffed half a banana into his mouth. Mrs Singh clicked her tongue in disapproval. 'If only you got up when you were called, there wouldn't be all this rush.' She straightened a chair. 'Every breakfast it's the same.' She bent over the table and took away his plate.

'Your father will be hard at work already,' she chided. 'And this morning, there's another elephant gone lame for him to worry about.' She bustled inside the house.

A scarlet cardinal bird flew across the verandah and landed at the far end of the table. It put its head on one side and regarded Himal with a speculative eye. The boy pushed a piece of bread towards it. His chair scraped as he stood up. The bird seized the bread and flew up into the branches of a nearby mango tree. 'Well at least he's happy,' thought Himal.

He looked out over the garden. The early morning air was fresh and the ground smelt damp. Two broken snail-shells lay on the concrete path below. 'Clever things, birds,' he thought and wondered when the thrushes had first learnt to use the concrete path as a tool. Not unlike humans and a tin-opener. Guaranteed easy access. Instant snail! Something like that.

His mother popped her head out of the kitchen. Then came out, waving her hands at him. 'Himal! Those trousers are a disgrace. Look at all that dust. Go and brush them this minute!' She started slapping at his legs.

'No, Mum! Stop it! Here I'll do it!' he told her and backed rapidly away.

'You should be setting a better example,' she told him. 'Especially when, when…' She didn't finish the sentence. She didn't need to. Himal knew exactly what she meant. *Especially when your father becomes Chief Inspector and is permanently in charge of everything here in the Tiger Park.*

'Come on, Himal!' Anji called from the garden. 'I'm going without you.'

He swore under his breath, grabbed his bag and rushed down the steps after her.

'I'll be so amazingly glad when Dad gets this promotion,' he grumbled, as they began the mile-long walk to the tarmac road. He kicked at a loose stone. 'I mean he's bound to get it this time, isn't he? He gets on with everyone. He knows what he's doing. So what's the problem? I don't know how much more I can take of all this fuss.'

Anji frowned. 'Mum's the worst,' she said. 'It's not Dad's fault. He's pretty laid back about everything, considering. She bit my head off too this morning.' They walked in silence for the next few minutes, past clumps of bamboo and straggly rows of wild sugar cane, aware of the day brightening as the sun rose behind them.

'It's all this tension and stuff,' Himal complained. 'It's getting worse and worse! I wake up in the morning and I'm still totally stressed out.

And this week's the worst it's ever been. When's it going to end?' He shook his head. At thirteen, Himal was big for his age and already as tall as his parents. Anji was a head shorter and a year younger than him.

Both of them were usually easy-going individuals with ready smiles for everyone. But not today. 'It'll be like this until Dad knows if he's passed the promotion board,' Anji said. 'Remember? He didn't get it the first time. And they only meet twice a year to consider people.'

Himal clapped a hand to his forehead. 'Six more months! You're joking!'

Anji looked at him and sighed. 'You're a real old drama queen, aren't you? You could walk into Bollywood tomorrow and they'd give you a job on the spot. You know there was a promotion board in Delhi last week. Mum's been going on and on about it.' She shook her head impatiently. 'That's why it's so bad right now. They're waiting to hear. So just keep your fingers crossed. And stop being so theatrical!'

A thought occurred to her. She looked at him and said innocently, 'This reminds me of when you were waiting to be picked for that cricket team. You made an awful fuss about that too.'

'Huh!' said Himal, ignoring her remark. 'Well, all this stuff can't come too soon for me. It's like a great black cloud hanging over everything.'

Anji thought for a moment then brightened. 'Hey! It's Saturday tomorrow. We'll be with the elephants! And Dev's promised us a ride. Cheer up. It's not all bad!'

They turned a bend in the track and saw a group of people some way ahead of them. 'Come on!' she cried. 'Let's catch 'em up.'

It felt good to run, Himal decided. Almost as if he was leaving his problems behind him, at home. He spotted his best friend, Yogi, walking a little way behind the others. He had his head buried in a book. Himal grinned. He raced up behind the boy, grabbed him by the shoulders and spun him round towards the monsoon ditch that ran beside the track.

'Snake!' he shouted in mock horror. 'Look out! Snake!'

Yogi teetered at the edge, his arms windmilling

wildly. A quick push, then Himal was running with the rest of them, all the way to the main road.

As they got there, an old bus with wooden slats in the windows came into sight. It had once been painted in bright bands of green and blue and bright yellow. Now, the faded sides were streaked with rust and there were patches of red lead along the bottom. They clambered on board cheerfully, greeting and calling to the other children from the Park, who had got on earlier.

The seats were hard and narrow and were so close together, Himal had to sit at an angle to get comfortable. 'What's the book, Yogi?' he demanded with a grin, as his friend came breathlessly down the aisle towards him.

Yogi glared at him. 'It's about cockroaches and other pests. I'll lend it to you. You'll enjoy it.' He flopped on to the seat opposite. Yogi's father was in charge of the equipment stores at the Park. It was a place Himal loved to visit. It was like being in a huge cave, stacked with mysterious objects and smelling of leather, rope and old animal sweat.

The driver shouted at them to sit down. The bus backfired and clattered off in a cloud of oily exhaust. It lurched into a pothole and the whole bus shook. Someone bit their tongue and yelled. The driver smiled and crashed the gears. Himal sat with his back against the side of the bus and a foot braced against the seat in front of him. Then he resigned himself to the hour-long journey to Amra and their school.

7

The cubs' first brush with death began innocently enough. There had been a very heavy dew before dawn and the grass was sodden. Deep in the forest, there was so much moisture dripping from the leaves that it could have been raining. The cubs' fur was soaking. Taza and Phur found a flat rock to stretch out on close to a clump of trees and lay there feeling miserable. Poga sat on her tail some distance away and groomed herself.

As the sun grew stronger, the ground began to steam. Poga did not pay it much attention at first. Soon, though, a dense mist rolled silently towards her and started blotting out trees and bushes. Poga stood up and stared around, puzzled. A moment later, there was no sign of the others at all.

She was surrounded by a silent white cloud that reduced her world to a small, dripping bubble. There was nothing to see. No birds or monkeys to be heard. Nothing. Just this great spider's web closing in on her. She snarled at it to keep away. It swirled even closer. Her paw leapt out, claws unsheathed as she struck. She tried to bite it but her teeth found nothing. She jumped to one side. The mist followed. Alarmed, she backed away.

She took a deep breath and roared as loudly as she could. The sound fell flat at her feet. She listened and thought she heard one of the others answering. But couldn't be sure. Then she heard another roar, only this time coming from the opposite direction.

Confused, she took another step sideways, and another. Nothing happened. She sprang forward and made a sudden dash, head down through the shifting walls of mist. She ran for ten or more metres – it was impossible to tell how far – then realised it was not going to let her through. When she stopped, it wrapped itself even more tightly around her. Her coat was sodden and she was shivering with cold. She sat down and howled for Kuma.

After a few minutes, Poga stopped, deciding that this strange thing would be affecting her mother as well. She shook herself and decided to wait and catch the mist off guard. She sat like a statue, eyes half closed to keep out the glare. Then, she took a deep breath and ran! How long for, she had no idea. Inside the bubble, time did not exist. There was no sensation of it passing. There was no way of measuring anything. She thought she was running uphill but could not be certain. She had no way of judging how fast she was covering the ground.

She saw a rock loom out of the mist ahead and dodged to one side. Other rocks were showing and she slowed to a walk, picking her way between them. Only then did it occur to her that the mist was thinning. Trees were appearing, grey shadows with golden tops. And then she was out in the sunlight and a wave of warmth and colour poured over her, swamping her senses.

Poga rolled over and over in sheer exuberance,

snatching at the grass with her teeth and spitting it out when it tickled her nose. She wriggled on her back, kicking her feet at the sun and growling at it in mock ferocity.

Thirty minutes later, the mist had all gone. Not a wisp remained. Sucked dry by the sun as if it had never existed. She stared down at the forest and then out to the bare plains beyond. She was close to the top of a hill. A vertical wall of rock some thirty metres high towered above her. There were other hills dotted around but none she recognised. Below her, the forest was a vast sweep of treetops. There was nothing familiar anywhere. And no sign of the others. For the very first time in her life she was alone.

She put her head back and looked up at the sky and caught sight of a dozen or more crows circling. She almost fell over in excitement. That could only mean one thing. There was a kill somewhere down there. And a very recent one because there were no vultures there yet. Kuma must have pulled it down!

Poga growled in triumph. She ran backwards and forwards in short rushes, trying to spot exactly where the kill was. She watched the crows swooping down. They did not stay long on the ground so she reasoned Kuma must still be there, feeding. There was a stream close to the kill. She could see it gleaming brightly in the sun. She was sure now she knew where it was. Bursting with excitement, she leapt down the hillside.

She ran easily through the forest. In front of her, a herd of chital deer took to their heels, their scuts bobbing in alarm. Langur monkeys swung through the trees, screeching at her. Poga was exhilarated. Nothing she had done in her short life had prepared her for this intense enjoyment of power. She ran faster, longing now to find Kuma and fling herself upon her.

There was the stream in front of her. A stream she recognised. She cast around and soon found Kuma's scent on a low bush. There were her mother's pugmarks in the sand and several smaller tracks that must belong to the other cubs. She was back in Kuma's home range. She was safe.

Happily, she looked around and recognised other familiar things. The banyan tree where she had last played with Taza. A large black stone on the stream bottom. She bent and drank quickly. She was very close to where Kuma had left them before the mist had come down. She wondered if the other cubs were still waiting there.

She hesitated for a moment. Should she find the others and wait with them? Memories of the mist came swirling back. Of being lost and just a little bit frightened. She shivered and shook out her fur. No! She wanted her mother. She jumped over the stream and began to run. There was a clump of mango trees ahead with black branches and dark green, glossy leaves. An elderly buzzard was flying over the top of them. Poga could hear the bones in its wings, creaking. The kill could not be far away.

She thought she heard snarling and ran towards the sound. She leapt up a steep bank and pushed her way through a fringe of young bamboo. Without thinking, she ran out into the open.

8

A dead chital doe lay half eaten on the ground. Standing over it, were five of the most feared predators in the forest. Wild dogs. They were the size of Alsatians but with shorter legs and much wider muzzles. They were a deep red in colour with black, bushy tails that stuck out behind them. Their jaws were covered in blood.

Poga had only ever seen them at a distance but she knew at once that she was in danger. Great danger. Kuma had several times warned the cubs about wild dogs. They lived in disciplined packs of up to twelve adults. Sometimes, they would combine with other packs and hunt really big prey, like buffalo or guar. Every animal in the forest feared them. Even tigers.

They were the most intelligent and remorseless hunters of all. They were the only animals that could chase a tiger off its kill, if there were enough of them. Once the pack found its prey, they would chase it all day and, if necessary, all night. They could run at a fast trot over long distances without any signs of tiredness. When the prey was exhausted and cornered, they would circle round then attack from all sides, simultaneously. The animal would be eaten in minutes because wild dogs could gulp down four kilos of meat each, every sixty seconds.

Kuma had warned the cubs never to try and take a kill away from them. She once saw a big male leopard confronting a single pair of dogs. In no time at all, the rest of the pack came running up and surrounded the leopard. The leopard managed to kill four of them before the pack pulled it down. It was something Kuma had never forgotten. And now, Poga was facing five of them!

The cub snarled, instinctively opening her mouth wide to bare her teeth. In an adult tiger, it would have been a frightening gesture. A warning to back away, fast. The pack leader looked across at her, calculating. He noticed her lack of canines and body size. He barked once at the others then put his head down and started tearing at the deer again. Poga waited, uncertain. The dogs were swallowing great chunks of meat at an amazing speed. They seemed to be totally ignoring her. She took a step backwards. Not one of them looked up. She took another and felt the bamboo behind her. She turned and fled.

Poga knew now where she was in the forest. She turned and headed for the place where the family had been earlier that morning. But she hadn't gone more than a couple of hundred metres when something made her stop and look back. The dogs were following her. They were running at an easy pace and strung out in an extended line. Poga's heart raced. There could be no mistake. They were after her!

In disbelief, she ran for her life! Faster than she had ever run before. She jumped high over the stream to miss the damp sand and raced across a clearing. Only then did she become aware of the commotion. The trees were full of monkeys jeering at her. They swung through the branches trying to keep up and screaming after her. Crows measured the distance between herself and the pack, then swooped low over her head, calling in delight.

Poga snatched another look back. The dogs were much closer. She could see their tongues hanging from the sides of their mouths. The dogs at each end of the line were running faster than the others. The next moment, she realised why. They were encircling her. Closing in and distracting her while the rest of the pack caught up. Her heart lurched. She felt helpless. She didn't know what to do. She was tiring. Another hundred metres, not much more, and then she must rest. Her breath was coming in ragged gasps. Her chest was aching.

Then she saw the place where Kuma had left them. She recognised the shape of the trees. And there was the flat rock where Taza and Phur had been. She bounded towards it, calling loudly for help. But there was no one there. They had all gone. And she was utterly on her own.

A dog appeared running across the flat rock

close to her. And another. Now, there were dogs everywhere. On either side. And one behind her! It bit at her back leg. She spun round, snarling. Quick as a flash, another dog attacked. She stumbled and felt its teeth tearing at her flesh. Poga gasped at the pain. She swivelled and hit it with her paw. But the dog had its muzzle buried in her belly and its head was jerking from side to side.

There was a dog snapping at her nose. Her eyes swam. She couldn't see. More pain. Teeth were ripping at her throat. The sounds of growling were changing to a triumphant howl. Two dogs were yanking at her back legs, trying to pull her over. There was a roaring in her ears. She staggered, fighting to stay on her feet. The dogs were leaping over her back. She smelt the stink of their breath and then her legs gave way and she fell into the middle of the pack.

And as she did so, Kuma erupted from out of nowhere. Before the dogs knew what was happening, she seized the leader in her jaws and crushed his skull with one massive bite. Roaring with rage, she charged two of the dogs, catching one of them a tremendous blow with her paw.

There was a sound like a breaking stick and the dog howled and began to drag itself away. The rest of the pack fled with Kuma in furious pursuit.

By the time she returned, Poga's breath was coming in shallow gasps. Kuma licked the cub's face and the wounds on her legs and neck. But there was nothing she could do about the great hole in her side where the ribs had been bitten back. Kuma waited while the life force drained from Poga's body. She nuzzled her ears and rubbed Poga's face with her own. She mewed at her cub, encouraging her to live. Poga opened her eyes wide and began to shiver. Then the pain went out of them and her head flopped on to the ground.

Kuma walked slowly away, leaving her cub to the scavengers. She found the old watercourse and grunted for the others to join her. They came running up, delighted to see her and looking for affection. Kuma stood listening, wondering where the rest of the pack might be. They would show her no mercy if they found her. She stank of their blood. It was the cubs leaping up at her mouth that decided her. She led them at a fast trot out of the forest and up the steep hillside to the cave where they had been born. Until the wild dogs had gone, she would not risk hiding them anywhere else.

9

The alarm clock jingled. A hateful, insistent sound that brought the boy out of a satisfying dream. He stretched out a hand and fumbled to switch it off. The noise stopped and Himal's eyes blinked open. The dream was gone. Only the barest memory of it survived. He lay there trying hard to find it again but failed. The house seemed very quiet. Perhaps his parents had overslept. He smiled. Now wouldn't that be a laugh!

He sat up and stretched. Then remembered. It was the weekend! And the joke was on him! So there was no rush. No stress. He could lie in until eight o'clock and after that, there were the elephants to help with! Every Saturday, he and

Anji spent the day in the stables doing whatever odd jobs the elephant-drivers, or mahouts, asked them to. It was the very best part of the week. He sank back into bed and pulled the sheet up to his nose. He wiggled his toes. Life at times could be really good.

After breakfast, he and Anji got on their bicycles and began the long ride to the stables. Mrs Singh worried about them coming face to face with a tiger or a leopard and never really believed her husband's reassurances. They were, after all, cycling through the forest.

Himal and Anji had only once met an animal on the track and that had been a sloth bear. It had ambled across in front of them, about twenty metres away, but gave no sign of seeing them. They often heard monkeys chattering and occasionally spotted one in the branches. But that was all. The only place they didn't like passing was an old tree where there was a hornets' nest. They always pedalled much harder here. If the forest ever felt spooky, as it did sometimes, they would call out to one another or laugh loudly.

Twenty minutes later, they reached Park

Headquarters and cycled past the old parade ground. Outside their father's office, the flag drooped. It was going to be another hot, airless day. Anji wiped her brow. A little further on, where the road went steeply downhill towards the high stone walls of the stables, she sat up straighter and enjoyed the rush of air on her face.

The mahouts and their families lived in grass thatched houses grouped together in neat lines, outside the main gate to the stables. The houses all had yellow walls and brightly coloured doors. There were banana trees in every garden and red canna lilies grew wild. There were volleyball nets strung between palm trees and groups of children playing intently.

On Saturday mornings, there was a small market. It was already bustling with people. There were stalls selling peppers and onions and piles of mangoes. Nearby, a man was cooking curry over a glowing charcoal fire. The smell of garlic and coriander climbed into the sky. A woman was selling hot, sweet tea from a battered urn. Anji waved to her. She grinned, called them over and thrust sticky yellow cakes into their hands.

Chickens pecked in the dust. Bicycle bells jingled as their riders wobbled in and out of the crowd. Children ran everywhere and a very young elephant stood beside a banana tree, quietly helping itself.

Himal grinned. He loved this place and all its noise and colour. He wished his own family lived here and were part of it. At the gates of the stables, they dismounted. No bikes or vehicles were allowed in. Some years ago, a lorry had backfired, upsetting an elephant. The elephant ran amok and did a lot of damage.

Their father's oldest friend, Dev Patel, greeted them cheerfully. He was the senior mahout and in charge of all the elephants. He and Inspector Singh had been boy mahouts together. They had grown up in the Park, looking after elephants and learning the ways of the forest. Dev had chosen to stay with the animals while Inspector Singh, encouraged by his wife, had slowly risen through the ranks. Dev was a small man, not much bigger than Anji, but his personality and sense of humour dominated everything.

'Your father's got a party of "high-ups" from

Delhi visiting on Monday. So everyone's got to work twice as hard today,' he told them with a wink.

'What shall we do first?' Himal asked.

Dev scratched his cheek. 'Well, seeing it's you,' he said thoughtfully, 'why not do what you're naturally best at.' He turned and pointed to a large wheelbarrow. 'See that?' he asked. 'Take it to the stables. Pick up a shovel and start mucking out!' He roared with laughter and gave Himal's shoulder a rough squeeze. 'Keep an eye on him, Anji,' he called. 'And don't let him fall down on the job.'

'And what can I do?' she asked, smiling broadly.

'Bring in fresh bedding and start laying it when your brother finishes.' He went off still chuckling.

Anji grinned. 'Come on,' she said. 'It'll give us an appetite for lunch!'

The stables were large and airy with a stall for every elephant. There were twelve mature females, who carried out the patrol duties, and a further seven juveniles and calves. They all had different personalities and their own place in a well-ordered hierarchy. Between them they produced five tons of dung a day.

Himal trundled the barrow across the yard while Anji went off to the feed shed. Inside the stables, the air was full of the musky smell of elephants and the pungent stink of ammonia. Himal knew from experience that some mornings the smell of urine was so strong, it made his eyes water.

There were shouts of greeting from the mahouts already working there. Himal waved back and selected an empty stall. He hung his shirt on a post and took a deep breath. He slid the shovel into the heap and set to work. It was like cutting into a very big fruit cake and soon sweat was running down his neck.

Ten minutes later, he had filled his first barrow. Behind the stables, there was a huge dung-heap which had accumulated over many years. It was sixty metres long and almost as wide. Flocks of sparrows quarrelled and pecked over it. Every now and then, a hawk would come plummeting down from a dazzling sky and seize one. Then it would fly to the top of a nearby tree and eat it.

As Himal approached he began stamping his feet. Dev had told him a long time ago that this was a way of scaring away any snakes that might be lurking. Last year, there had been a rumour that a pair of king cobras was making a nest there. Everyone had believed it at the time because the heap was full of harmless rat snakes. King cobras only ate snakes and rat snakes were their favourite. The scare lasted for many months. So far this year, no one had brought it up again. Perhaps, it had only been a rumour after all, thought Himal. He certainly hoped so!

When he finished mucking out the stall, he went to find Dev.

'Good. Now you can have some fun,' Dev told him. 'I want you to wash down the floor in there. You know where the hose is.'

Himal knew from his father, that elephants liked a clean place to live.

'They won't lie down on a filthy surface. And they won't drink dirty or stagnant water,' Inspector Singh had said.

Anji meanwhile had strewn fresh bedding in three different stalls and was panting from the effort. Her hair was full of grass seed and there were pieces of straw down her back. She went over to Himal and splashed water over her face and arms. Then she helped him finish.

A mahout asked them to help wash an elderly female. They took it in turns to play the water hose up and down her sides, while the others scrubbed hard. The old elephant enjoyed every moment. She stood with her eyes closed, making little crooning noises of pleasure. Occasionally, she lifted her trunk and sprayed water over them – and smiled when she had done so. But it was shoulder-breaking work and Himal and Anji were very glad when she was eventually led away.

Just before noon, the first of the forest patrols returned. Anji and Himal heard the excited cries of the village children and the calls of the mahouts as they went past the houses. As the patrol swung in through the gates, a baby elephant ran squealing to its mother and immediately started to feed.

The mahouts slid down their elephants' legs on to the ground and the stables were suddenly full of people laughing and calling to one another. Anji and Himal watched the men undo the wide girth strap that ran under the elephants' belly and carefully ease the wooden howdah off its back.

Dev joined them. 'Well done, you two. That was good work.' A thought seemed to strike him. He snapped his fingers 'I know what I meant to ask. What do you think about your father going to speak to your school?'

They looked at him blankly.

He shrugged. 'Perhaps I am mistaken. Never mind. Would you like to ride out, this afternoon?'

He grinned at their enthusiasm. 'Well then, let's go and eat in the market. Then we can get started.'

They walked together through the main gate. 'I want to show you something special today,' Dev told them. 'A fine tiger. An old acquaintance you might say. And she's got three big cubs with her. I've been watching her for some time and I think I know where she'll be this afternoon.'

10

'Dad! Is it true you're coming to talk to our school?' Himal asked.

The Singh family was eating supper in the kitchen. A pressure lamp hung from a hook, hissing quietly. Its light bathed the room in a yellow glow and threw their shadows swooping and tumbling across the walls and ceiling. The Singhs did have electricity but it was unreliable and frequently failed at crucial moments – often when Mrs Singh was in the middle of baking. They preferred the lamp. It felt more friendly.

At night, the windows were covered with mesh screens to keep out the mosquitoes. It was Himal's job to clip them into place just before sunset. By now, an hour after dusk, hundreds of insects and moths were clinging to the outside, drawn there by the light.

In the forest beyond, the night creatures hunted or hid. Their squeaks and slitherings and occasional screams were drowned by the croaking of toads and the incessant screech of grasshoppers. There was not a light to be seen anywhere, even though there were six identical bungalows within a hundred-metre radius of them. The bungalows housed the senior staff of the Park.

In addition to the Singhs, Dev Patel and his family lived here. They had the next bungalow along. Beyond them lived the Inspector's other good friend, known to everyone as Joshi. He was a large, jolly man who ran the stores. He looked after the different needs of the tigers, elephants and humans who lived in the Park. His son, Yogi, was Himal's friend.

The house on the other side of the Singhs was empty. The sudden death of the previous Park Commander, some months ago, meant that Inspector Singh was now in charge. Whether or not he would stay as such, and gain the necessary promotion, was still causing a great deal of tension at home.

Mrs Singh put a heavy pan down on the table and took off the lid. 'Pass your plate, Anji,' she said.

Anji wasn't listening. She was looking at her father with shining eyes. 'Dad! Are you really coming to talk to our school? That's fantastic.'

'What are you going to talk about?' Himal asked.

Inspector Singh reached for a lime pickle. He shook his head in surprise. 'Hey! Wait a moment!' he told them. 'I only agreed to do it yesterday. How did you know about that?'

'Pass your plate, Anji,' Mrs Singh ordered.

Anji turned with a frown. 'Oh, Mum! Not too much, please. I'm not that hungry.'

'Someone's got a very good bush telegraph,' Inspector Singh chuckled.

'You're a growing girl,' Mrs Singh said. 'You need all the nourishment you can get.' And she gave Anji an extra spoonful of lentils to make the point. She looked at her husband. 'You haven't told me anything about a speech.'

'Well I only heard myself yesterday morning,' he protested, taking a steaming plate from her. 'The headmaster telephoned and invited me to come and talk to them at next term's speech day.'

'What about?' Himal insisted.

'Not till then? But that's months away.' Anji sounded disappointed.

'You could take in that old chair and have it repaired,' Mrs Singh mused, handing Himal his helping.

Inspector Singh stared round at his family then smiled. 'I've been asked to talk about tigers. What else?'

They ate in silence for a while and Mrs Singh smiled in satisfaction. Himal asked for some more bread and began to mop his plate with it. He licked his fingers.

'You haven't mentioned poachers for a long time, Dad,' he said.

'Well, not for at least a month anyway,' Anji agreed.

Mrs Singh frowned. 'Don't tell me they're

starting up again. That's all we need. It was very bad last time.'

Anji and Himal looked at her. 'There was gunfire,' she told them. 'Three years ago. Your father was very brave.' She nodded at the memory to emphasise how bad it had been.

Himal's eyes widened. This was news to him.

'You were too young to understand,' she told him.

Himal looked at his father with interest. 'You expecting trouble, Dad?'

Inspector Singh frowned. 'There's no particular threat. But these people are always a menace. And they're much better organised these days.' He shifted in his chair. 'They could strike at any time and we might not even know about it for days, weeks even.'

'So are you going to talk about poachers, Dad?' Himal insisted.

Her father thought for a moment. 'Well, just a little, yes!'

'But what if they want to know a lot more about poaching? Like how much they get paid? Will you tell them that, too?' Himal challenged.

It was a discussion they had often had.

Inspector Singh hesitated. 'I'll give them some of the facts.'

'And when they ask you how you're combating them, what will you say?'

His father looked uncomfortable. 'I'll tell them we have trained forest guards, experts in their field.'

'It's the party line,' Mrs Singh stated. 'It's what your father has to say.'

'But it's a joke, Dad, isn't it?' Himal scoffed. 'We all know that. I mean, just a handful of mahouts looking after all that land! It's crazy!'

Inspector Singh flushed. 'Since you put it like that, then, yes! Perhaps it is! But I don't need you to tell me that, Himal. Tell the politicians!' He drummed his fingers on the kitchen table. 'You can sneer all you like but I'm the poor devil who's got to make it work. The fall guy, as you'd call it.'

He drained his glass of beer and looked hard at his son.

'I can't tell the public and the newspapers we've only got twelve elephants to patrol the whole damn park, now, can I? That'd be an open invitation to every poacher in India to come down here.'

Anji looked impressed. 'Will you be in the newspaper?'

'Of course he'll be,' said Mrs Singh. 'Your father is an important man.'

'And that's why I've got to be very careful what I say. I'll give them the facts and figures about tiger numbers and hope it registers.' Inspector Singh put his hand on his wife's wrist. 'Is there a little bit more?' he asked. 'That was delicious.'

Mrs Singh looked pleased. She scraped at the saucepan with a large wooden spoon.

'Mrs Patel was telling me yesterday,' she confided, 'that no one believes a word the government is saying about the number of tigers left in the wild.'

'It's less than four thousand,' Himal told her.

'And there were hundreds of thousands of them not that long ago,' said Anji sadly.

'That's the latest figure. Isn't it, Dad?' Himal asked. 'Four thousand tigers?'

A shadow crossed the Inspector Singh's face.

'It's a very optimistic one,' he said gloomily. They looked at him, surprised by his change of tone. He toyed with his spoon. 'If you want to know the real truth, the way things are going at the moment, they'll all be dead in ten years' time. Every one of them. Even the ones in zoos. There won't be a tiger left in India. Not according to some official figures I saw today.'

There was a shocked silence. Himal shook his head in confusion. What was his father saying? It was unbelievable. It had to be.

'All gone in ten years? You mean like, killed?'

Inspector Singh rapped the table with his knuckles. 'Please. No more questions! Not tonight. I don't want to talk about it.'

When he had finished eating, he laid his fork and spoon down on the plate.

'I need some night air,' he said. 'I might just go and have a game of dominoes with Dev.' Then to Mrs Singh, 'I may be a little late. Don't wait up for me.' He gave them all a fleeting smile and stood up.

Himal and Anji stared at each other in disbelief, their faces rigid with shock.

'No tigers left?' Anji gasped. 'Dad! You can't mean that!'

But Inspector Singh did not reply. The screen door shut behind him with a bang.

11

It was the hot season once again. The monsoon had come and gone. For three months since the last rains fell, the ground was covered with rich new grass. For the deer and antelopes, it was the time for giving birth. For tigers, it was a time of excess.

Hundreds of deer joined together to form even bigger herds for mutual protection while they dropped their calves on the dusty ground. Hunting was easy. And if Kuma failed to bring down an adult chital, there several long-legged youngsters within easy reach.

The cubs grew quickly. Taza now weighed close to ninety kilos and was almost as big as his mother.

Phur was considerably smaller. Both cubs were strong enough to pull down a female chital or a barking deer but they still lacked the killer bite. They would be dependent on Kuma for some time yet. At twelve months old, they were beginning their transition to adult life and Kuma was teaching them the skills they would need to survive on their own.

So now they watched the prominent white spot at the back of each ear, as she moved silently through the grass, towards her unsuspecting prey. They saw how carefully she selected her approach route. How she used any folds in the ground, tussocks of grass or ant-hills, for concealment. How she could stand motionless for minutes, hardly seeming to breathe. They noted the lengths she went to and the patience needed to get as close as possible to the prey.

At first they were puzzled why she would stand up and break off an attack if spotted. But they quickly found out why. In their first attempts at stalking, both cubs broke cover far too soon and ran flat out after their fleeing prey. But tigers, like domestic cats, have poor stamina. A fast chase over two hundred metres left the cubs panting and often winded. They learnt the hard way that unless they got within thirty metres of the target, there was not a deer in the forest that could not outrun them.

Kuma taught them many other things. They learnt how langur monkeys and chital deer worked together to give the forest its most effective warning system. Chitals gathered under the trees where the monkeys fed. The langurs were careless eaters and dropped fruit or leaves which the deer eagerly ate. From the treetops, the monkeys kept a constant lookout for tigers which protected the chitals while they fed. When the langurs swung down on to the ground, looking for grubs and the insects, the deer kept watch for them.

The cubs learnt to roll in buffalo or elephant dung if hunting the barasingha swamp deer. These deer had the sharpest sense of smell of any animal. If the wind was right, they could scent a tiger from hundreds of metres away.

The way the cubs played was changing. There was less good-natured sparring. Instead, they seized each other by the throat, copying the way

Kuma killed the great sambar stags. At the kills themselves, they examined the deep puncture marks on the animal's necks and tried to cover them with their own jaws.

They discovered more about the other predators they shared the forest with. One hot, still afternoon, the cubs heard Kuma's warning growl. Taza and Phur were lying in the stream, their eyes closed in lazy contentment. The growl brought them to their feet, alert and snarling. Kuma called them to her and together they stood looking down and studying a leopard's pugmarks.

By the size of them and the round shape of each individual toe, Kuma knew it was a male. And the absence of any deep cracks in the pad, told her that it was still quite young. The cubs examined the tracks and carefully smelt them. They began to track it and soon found its scent mark on a bush. Kuma grunted, backed into the bush and sprayed it with her own.

They climbed up through the forest towards a jumble of boulders high above them. Taza found a leopard's claw marks scored deep into the bark of a tree. Some of them he saw were very recent, judging by the colour of the wood beneath.

Moments later, Kuma halted, listening. Then the cubs heard it too. A big animal was coming towards them. The next moment, a pair of pheasants erupted out of the undergrowth, screeching in panic. A big leopard followed, bounding through the bushes with a monkey in its jaws.

It saw the tigers at exactly the same moment and flattened itself. Kuma knew from long experience that leopards could size up a situation faster than any other forest creature. She sprang at it. But in that brief second, the leopard made a leap for the nearest tree and was swarming up into its branches, still holding the monkey.

Kuma roared and shook the tree with her paws. The leopard stared down with blazing eyes. Phur leapt as high as she could, gripped the trunk with her claws and started to climb. The leopard watched her for a moment, then ran smoothly up into the top branches. It still held the monkey. It saw Phur's claws slip and knew the tiger's weight would pull it down. Phur fell, twisted in midair, and landed on her feet.

Baffled, the tigers paced up and down, growling and threatening. But they knew, as the leopard did, there was nothing more they could do. As long as the leopard stayed where it was, it was safe. In the end, Kuma grunted bad-temperedly and led them away.

The other creatures Kuma warned them about were snakes. The very next day, Phur spotted a snake gliding across the ground. She chased after it and playfully brought her paw down hard on its tail. With bewildering speed, the snake turned and struck at her. She leapt to one side with a startled yowl but not before the snake struck again. She stared after it as it slipped into a crack in the ground. Then she noticed the drops of venom glistening on her fur.

Kuma cuffed her, angry at her stupidity. Had the fangs struck the thin skin of her nose, she might have died. Snakes were best avoided at all times. Pythons could be hunted but only by a fully-grown tiger. A five-metre-long python was a dangerous predator. They often waited along the branch of a tree overhanging a well-used trail. As an animal passed underneath, the python flung itself down, taking advantage of its own weight and their shock to wrap itself around them. Its main weapon was the terrible crushing power of its coils. There were not many animals that could break out of a full-grown python's embrace. And a big python would not hesitate to take on a twelve-month-old tiger, if hungry enough.

In Kuma's experience, there were two sorts of snake. There were those who crushed their prey, and the others, that lay in wait and killed them with a bite. One day, it might be vital for the cubs to know the difference. So she took the cubs out on to the plains where the ground was deep in dust, and soon found what she was looking for.

She knew that poisonous snakes waited for their prey to come to them and because of this, they had no need to travel fast. In fact, they moved over the ground quite slowly. But to travel like this, a snake had to wriggle a great deal. So those tracks made up of a lot of short curves were almost certainly made by cobras or vipers. Like the one Phur had teased.

By contrast, snakes which chased their prey, like rat snakes, were thin-bodied, active and fast movers. When they covered the ground, they left generally straight tracks. If there were ridges or dips in the ground, their bellies only brushed the high points.

But there was one special snake that Kuma wanted to warn the cubs about. It was not the most poisonous snake in the forest. In fact, its venom was less lethal than that of the common cobra. What made it so dangerous was its intelligence. That, and the sheer quantity of venom it delivered with each bite. Enough to kill an elephant. It was the only snake Kuma had ever met that had its own territory which it actively defended.

One morning, Kuma growled at the cubs to follow and to stay very close. She remembered there had been a pair of king cobras living in the bamboo forest. She had not visited the place for some time now, because of them. She led the cubs past the flat rock, across the stream and along an almost dried up watercourse. They stopped only once, to drink at a puddle. A cloud of small blue butterflies swirled around their heads. Phur swatted at them with her paw. Afterwards, she looked back and saw them settling again.

Kuma leapt up a crumbling earth bank and stopped. The ground in front of her was covered with old bamboo leaves. They were dry and twisted and looked like snakes themselves. They rustled menacingly as the tigers walked past.

The hair on Kuma's spine lifted. She stopped twenty metres from a bush and gave a low growl. It was Taza who saw the king cobra first. He took a half-step back in surprise as a huge snake reared up. Its head was the same size as a fully grown monkey's. It swayed for a moment then put its head on one side and began to examine them. Its eyes were bright and quick to note any movement. The cubs growled deep in their throats, aware of its menace.

Kuma snarled at them to stay put. She took a deliberate step towards the snake, then another. The cobra's eyes fixed on her. It rose even higher and as they watched, they saw the skin on either side of its neck inflate into a large hood.

The next moment the cobra was gliding towards Kuma, its head, held back like a spring, ready to strike. Kuma felt its hatred. The hood was fully extended. This snake did not hiss like other snakes. Instead, it made a low, growling sound, more like a dog. It towered over the tigress, its eyes glittering. Kuma stepped back. The snake followed. The cubs now saw its full length. It was close to four metres long.

Another head appeared above the bushes. It was the female. One look and she immediately extended her hood and came straight for the tigress. She brushed past her mate, moving very quickly. Kuma scrambled back, hesitated, then turned tail and ran. The cubs bumped into each other in their fright to get away. The snakes watched them go, swaying together like dancers, until the tigers were out of sight. Only then did they drop back to the ground.

Kuma shook out her fur and pretended to groom herself. The cubs sat down and did the same. The cobra's aggression had shaken Kuma. And she knew the cubs were just as frightened. It was a good lesson to have learned.

It was while they were making their way back to the stream, that Kuma smelt wood smoke. She stiffened in alarm. Smoke meant only one thing. The thing that every single creature living in the forest dreaded. Somewhere close, the forest was on fire!

12

Kuma hesitated. Her first reaction was to flee but then she realised that until she knew where the fire was, she could be taking the cubs into greater danger. She tested the air and found the smoke had a very pungent scent to it. It was not a smell she knew. She waited, uncertain what to do next. There was something strange about this fire. It wasn't just the odd smell, there was something missing.

She remembered the last great fire when entire parts of the forest disappeared in a scorching wave of flame. It devoured clumps of trees whole, the flames leaping from tree to tree like demented monkeys. She could still hear the fire's great crackling roar and the sound of trees exploding, as their sap reached boiling point. The sky was black from smoke and falling ash. The noise was terrifying.

A lone bull elephant had been caught when the wind changed direction. She remembered the agonised screams when he realised he was cut off. Then the fire rolled over him and nothing more was ever heard or seen.

So what was happening now? Puzzled, Kuma swished her tail. What were the other animals doing? And the birds? Why was everything so normal? Where were all the panic-stricken cries? And the smoke was not getting any stronger. Gradually she relaxed but her curiosity was fully aroused. Calling the cubs to follow, she set out to investigate. A hundred metres further on, she stopped. There were elephants coming. And humans! She sank down beside a tree overlooking a game trail and waited.

The elephants came into view. The leader was plucking leaves and stuffing them into its mouth. There was a man sitting up on its head. The second elephant was about ten metres behind. As they got closer, Kuma saw the man pointing at her. He half stood up and called to the man on the elephant behind. They chattered loudly, like langurs. Kuma snarled and the cubs did the same.

As the first elephant came abreast, it tossed a branch at her. Kuma growled. The mahout's feet kicked the elephant's ears. There was a leathery, slapping sound. For an instant, Kuma looked directly into the man's eyes. Then they were past. As the second elephant came abreast, it trumpeted in derision and dropped dung. Kuma watched the men looking back at her and waited until they had disappeared into the forest, before leaping down on to the track. The cubs ran to the dung balls and examined them. Then they bounded after her.

Kuma had not forgotten the smoke and was hurrying on. They were now crossing into an unknown part of the forest. One she did not visit very often. This was her half-sister's territory and they began to find her scent marks on bushes and rocks. The forest was different here. Huge teak trees towered forty metres above their heads. There were birds everywhere. Golden orioles and crested drongos flew among the trees. Peacocks sat on low branches, their tail feathers hanging below them in shimmering veils of blue and green. Laughing thrushes were turning up dead leaves on the forest floor, looking for grubs. And all the time, the scent of wood smoke grew stronger.

There was something else too. More voices. Human voices. There were men calling to one another. Kuma hissed at her cubs and went forward on her own. Her great paws made no sound as they crossed the deep carpet of last year's leaves. The smell of smoke was very strong now. Her eyes were stinging. She stood motionless in a patch of grass, the stripes of her coat blending perfectly into this background. A tawny shadow, staring at the strange antics of the two men, barely thirty metres away.

13

The men were standing by the foot of a huge tree. One was looping a rope around his waist. The other was lashing together bunches of leaves into a two-metre-long, cigar-shaped bundle. Both of them were barefoot and wore old cotton shirts, buttoned at the wrist. Their trousers were ragged. The first man had a machete stuffed into his belt and a rolled-up canvas bag hanging from his waist. A spiral of grey smoke drifted up from a fire on one side of the tree.

The man who was about to climb was called Suresh. His companion was known as Hari. They had been friends since boyhood. They were wild honey gatherers, like generations of their families before them. They had grown up together in the forest and knew its ways. They were expert trackers and could find and follow even the most cunning leopard. They knew when a new tiger arrived to challenge for territory. And what the outcome was. But their greatest skill was stealing the honey from the scores of wild bee nests dotted around the forest.

While Suresh said a silent prayer to the spirits of the forest, Hari tied off the last bunch of leaves. He gave a grunt of approval as he pulled the cord tight. The leaves were long and crinkly-edged and if chewed, would numb the tongue and the inside of the mouth for several hours. The two men sold them in the marketplace in Amra, where they were much in demand as a remedy for toothache. Next, Hari picked up a paraffin-soaked rag and wiped it quickly over one end of the bundle. He dipped the end into the fire and held it there until the leaves began to smoulder. Soon, a cloud of pungent-smelling smoke was billowing upwards. He tied a length of thin rope around the other end and waited to hand it to Suresh.

Suresh slapped the palms of his hands on the

tree and looked up. Two rows of wooden pegs had been banged deep into the trunk. They curved high over his head and were lost to sight in the first layer of branches. Some of the pegs had recently been replaced. They looked new and frail against the roughness of the bark. He took the rope from Hari and wrapped it around his waist a couple of times. Then he spat on his hands, took a deep breath and began to climb.

Suresh climbed easily. His hands and feet seemed to curl around the pegs as he pulled himself smoothly upwards. The pegs looked almost too small to stand on. His arms were thin and stick-like but despite this, he was extremely strong. Soon, the first branches were just above his head. Seeing this he muttered to himself. He must concentrate. He must drive out all thoughts of his recent unhappy life. He must forget his wife and the trouble her wretched sister was causing. He shook his head again, angry with himself for being so easily distracted.

This was dangerous work. He had no fear of heights even though one slip from here would be his last. It was time now to concentrate entirely on what he was doing. It was only fair to Hari, his partner. Forty metres below, Hari called up to him. Suresh shouted back that he was fine. The nest was still some way above him. Ten metres? Not much more. It was six months since they had last visited this tree. So the nest would be bulging with honeycomb. He coughed and wiped his eyes on the back of his hand. Below him, the smouldering leaves swayed to and fro on their rope.

The first bees were brushing past his head to join the pattern of incoming insects. They held bright orange-coloured balls of pollen close to their bodies. He followed their flight and quickly spotted the nest. It hung on the side of the tree like some rare fruit, a metre long.

Suresh climbed to the next fork in the tree and squatted down. His toes and feet gripped the bark as he steadied himself. He hauled the bundle of leaves towards him, expertly turning it round so that the burning end now faced the nest. He took a couple of deep breaths to calm himself then edged out cautiously on to a thinner side branch.

Above him, the sound of the bees drove everything else from his mind. It was becoming a roar now like surf breaking on rocks. Millions and millions of bees circled there, blotting out the sun. Suresh moved forward, hanging on with fingers and toes, while he pushed the bundle in front of him.

The bees had caught the smell of smoke. Their buzzing deepened into panic-stricken rage as Suresh held the smoking leaves underneath the nest. For five long minutes, he remained motionless, while the smoke engulfed it, stupefying the bees. The dense, black swarm broke apart. Millions of bees grew giddy and lost all sense of direction.

Suresh was covered with them. They landed in his hair and tumbled out again, falling sixty metres to the ground where they crawled aimlessly for the next hour. Many stung him in their confusion but he barely noticed. He opened up the canvas sack so that it dangled securely by his knee. Then, taking out his machete, he began to cut large slices from the nest. The honey oozed and glistened like liquid gold. He worked steadily until the bag was full. By then, he had taken half the nest. He would leave the rest for the bees. They would rebuild and it would be there the next time he came to harvest.

Back on the ground, Hari covered the fire with handfuls of earth and stamped it down. He reached up for the canvas bag as it came jerking down and gave a cry of delight. He broke off a piece of the comb and ate it. His grin spread wider. 'The bees have been good to us!' he told Suresh. 'There must be a hundred rupees for both of us in here.'

Suresh shook his head and said sourly, 'And a hundred rupees is what rich people in Delhi will pay for just one small jar. But not to us. And we are risking our lives to get it for them!' He turned away and spat. Then asked, 'Know what I'll be doing when I get home?'

Puzzled, Hari shook his head.

'Collecting old cow dung to cook my supper on. That's what!'

'But that's women's work. That's for your wife to do,' Hari protested.

Suresh gave a short bitter laugh and shook his head. He stabbed his machete in the earth to clean it. Then said gloomily, 'Come on then. We'd better go before the bees wake up and find us.'

As the men's voices died away, Kuma ran forward towards the tree. Greedily, she began casting around, licking up loose fragments of honeycomb. The men walked on, unaware of the tiger so close behind them. Both wrapped in their own thoughts.

14

Hari stared at Suresh's back and shook his head. He had never seen his old friend so miserable. Normally, he was a cheerful, happy-go-lucky man, full of jokes and laughter. Something must have gone seriously wrong for him. They walked in silence through the forest, two canvas bags slung from the pole they were balancing on their shoulders. Dozens of chattering monkeys followed them, intrigued by the smell of honey.

Eventually, they reached a potholed road with drainage ditches on either side. Here they stopped and squatted down to wait for the first truck to Amra to come along. The town was twelve miles away and everyone who used the highway knew them and what they did for a living. Honey was a delicacy and an easy product to barter with, so they didn't have very long to wait.

Later, when they had finished bargaining and haggling, threatening and pleading with the owner of the factory who always took their honey, they went to the nearby market to celebrate. Each man bought sweet, milky tea. They sat at a glass-ringed table and shared a plate of sticky cakes. It was a ritual they had enjoyed for years. Normally, it was a time for laughter and fellowship.

Hari glanced at his friend. 'Well?' he challenged. 'That was a good price we got today. The best for a long time. You can't say it wasn't.' He was determined to get Suresh to cheer up. But to his horror, Suresh buried his head in his hands and gave a loud sob. Hari's jaw dropped. 'But what is wrong, old friend? Tell me! Please, tell me.'

Suresh sniffed loudly and shook his head. He stared down at the tabletop. 'I am tired of being poor,' he mumbled.

Hari blinked in surprise. He had certainly not expected this. He reached over and held Suresh's thin little wrist. 'People like us have always been poor,' he said. 'But there are many poorer still. Not everyone can sit at a table eating and drinking like this, can they?'

There was a silence. He leant towards his friend and his voice softened. 'You may be poor but you can still be happy. And you, Suresh, are usually very happy. So what has happened to you?'

Suresh looked away and saw a man in a faded cotton suit sit down at the table next to theirs. The suit was crumpled as if the man had travelled a long way in it. There were sweat patches at the armpits. He was a big, well-fed man who carried a briefcase. He looked important. The owner of the cafe himself came bustling up to take his order. And this seemed to confirm Suresh's worst fears. His fists clenched.

'Listen, and I'll tell you what is making me so distressed,' he told Hari. 'We agree that I am a poor man. My wife is the youngest daughter in a large family of girls. I took her with no dowry. She is very beautiful and I love her very much.'

Hari nodded encouragingly.

'Now her oldest sister is visiting and this woman is staying in a hotel here in Amra. A hotel!' Here,

Suresh banged the table with his fist. 'Compared to us, she is very rich. Her husband worked for the government and reached senior grade. Then he was killed in a car crash. Now she has a large compensation and is spending money like water.'

Suresh's voice thickened. 'Before she came,' he continued, 'my wife got ready the children's room for her to sleep in. She put wild flowers in a jar and spread fresh grass on the floor. We took the children into the room we use.' He shook his head at the memory. 'When she arrived, she told my wife she would not live in a shack. And why was there no running water? Then she saw my children drinking out of an old tin and she goes straight back to Amra, in the taxi.'

Hari stared at him and his heart began to melt for his old friend.

Suresh's voice rose. 'Now she is turning my wife against me. Filling her head with longing for things we can never afford. An electric stove, nice beds, television, even!' He laughed, bitterly. 'Why not an aeroplane too.'

Hari shook his head and gave a loud sigh. 'She is a disruptive, this sister!'

'There is worse,' Suresh told him. 'They both come here to the cinema in Amra, two times a week. And back again for shopping at weekends. She sends a taxi to pick up my wife. There and back! Last night there was no food ready for me! They were out buying new clothes.' He pushed his tea glass away. 'I am pleased she has new clothes to wear but it should be me who buys them for her.'

The big man in the suit stared at the canvas bags beside Hari's chair. He looked as if he was going to say something then changed his mind. Hari turned his attention back to his friend. 'Tell her to go. Get rid of her!' he said with a scowl.

Suresh looked even more miserable. 'She is not the sort of woman you can say that to. She has big city ways. She is clever with words. She makes me feel stupid. I don't want her to show me up in front of my wife.' He shook his head. 'She has a different pair of shoes for every day of the week. Imagine!'

He clasped his head again. 'That's why I say "if only I was rich". Never before have I ever really wanted to be. Now, I think about nothing else. It is like a sickness.'

'Excuse me,' said the man in the faded suit. 'But is that honey you've got in there?'

Hari nodded. 'Yes, Sir. But we've sold it already to the factory. They take all our honey.'

'Ah!' said the stranger, sounding interested. 'So you're honey gatherers, are you?' They looked at him and nodded. The stranger rubbed his hands together. 'Well, well, well. That's interesting. Very interesting.' He smiled at them. 'Perhaps I could interest *you* in something?' The smile broadened. 'You see, I'm starting up a new business myself, here in Amra. To supply the foreign export market. I'm going to need all sorts of forest products. The things rich people like.'

'Like what?' Suresh asked.

The man spread his hands. 'Oh! Things like good bamboo. For chairs and tables. And scented tree bark, sandalwood and certain pretty plants and flowers for decorations. Beautiful bird feathers. And wild honey of course. Lots of wild honey. I'd pay special rates for that.'

He fished in his pocket and produced a small

business card. 'You might just be the men I've been looking for. I need the best. And I pay the best. Far better rates than you've ever had in the past. Try me!'

Hari took the card and peered at it upside down.

'My name is Sam,' the man told them. 'Mister Sam. I'm opening a place by the railway station in the next few months. Come in when we're open. My people would enjoy talking to you.'

Hari kicked Suresh under the table. The two of them stared at each other.

'I have other interests as well,' Mr Sam told them. 'Up and down the country. You'd be joining a very successful company. Can I ask what your names are? Perhaps my manager can contact you?'

They told him.

'May I get you some more tea?'

Dumbfounded, they shook their heads.

Mr Sam looked at his watch. 'I must be on my way. I have to catch the night train to Rahlapore.' He got to his feet. 'The manager's name is Katni, by the way.' Then he was gone.

Suresh and Hari said nothing for a moment,

both waiting for the other to speak first. Then, 'Can't do any harm, I suppose?' said Suresh cautiously.

Hari grinned. 'No harm at all, my friend. No harm.'

15

Some days later, an official letter arrived at Park Headquarters. It was marked, 'Staff in Confidence' and addressed to 'Inspector Singh, Kanla National Tiger Park'. The postmark was Delhi.

This was it! thought Ambrose the chief clerk, gingerly holding it between his fingers. No doubt about it. The latest promotion list.

Before he handed it to the Inspector, Ambrose telephoned Joshi in the stores and Dev Patel at the elephant stables. 'It's arrived,' he told them. 'Come on over in the next half-hour and we'll celebrate.'

Inspector Singh was in his office. It was a happy, cluttered place that he greatly enjoyed. There were pictures of tigers and elephants and other animals on the walls. There was also a grainy, black and white photograph of two dead men lying on their backs. One had a bullet hole drilled through the middle of his forehead. They had been poachers and had killed ten tigers between them, to Inspector Singh's certain knowledge.

There was a battered table under one window. On it stood an old army radio set. In theory Headquarters could keep in touch with the elephant patrols anywhere in the Park. In practice, it was not so easy. All too frequently, hills or dense patches of forest blocked the signals. Sometimes, lightning and thunder interfered. More often, the distances involved proved too great and contact was lost. Even in the best of conditions, there were sometimes long delays between successful transmissions.

Inspector Singh had recently bought six mobile telephones. These, whilst not perfect, were certainly an improvement. He and Dev had one each and the remainder were allocated to the patrols.

It was a stiflingly hot morning and an elderly

electric fan clattered overhead. It pushed drafts of hot air from one side of the office to the other, without seeming to bother the small cloud of flies that hung there.

'Come in, Ambrose,' Inspector Singh called, seeing the man hovering in the open doorway. 'What have you got there?' Then he saw the grin on the other's face. 'Oh!' he said. 'Something important?'

The two men exchanged glances but said no more. Ambrose closed the door behind him and walked back along the wide verandah to his own office. Left alone, Inspector Singh took the letter and stared at it. His hands trembled. He turned it over a couple of times then, taking a deep breath, slid it open with a letter knife.

There was a single sheet of paper inside. He swallowed and pulled it out. His eyes darted to the bottom of the page. The names began to dance in front of his eyes but not before he saw several 'Singhs' listed there. He screwed his eyes shut, opened them, and began to read. His name was not there.

Perhaps they had mixed his initials up? Or put

them in the wrong order? He checked again. No! He said a silent prayer and this time his eyes flicked to the very top of the page. He mumbled the names out loud. He knew two of the men there. They were both younger than him and one of them, he was sure, had been to university. His finger stopped at the last name. There was no mistake. He had not been promoted this time either.

He groaned and laid his head on his arms. Disbelief, embarrassment and anger flooded through him. He stared at the desk top. Was it his age? Or his lack of any formal education? Soon, his friends would know and once again, he would have to accept their well-meant sympathy.

And then there was Mrs Singh. He'd better get that over with right away. She was going to be devastated. He felt suddenly remote from everything. Almost as if he was an actor on a stage, playing a part. In a daze, he folded the paper and slipped it into his shirt pocket. Outside, Ambrose was waiting, pretending to be reading a file. He came forward eagerly, but his smile died, when he saw Inspector Singh's face.

He watched him kick-start his moped and drive off.

'Damn it!' thought Ambrose. 'Damn it! Why is life so unfair to the good guys?'

16

Anji knew something was wrong when she saw her mother kneeling on the lawn. She was snipping at the grass with a pair of heavy clippers. School was over for another day and Anji was looking forward to getting home. Himal was some way behind her, fooling around with Yogi.

Anji frowned. The grass did not need cutting. It was brown and sparse and more bare earth than grass. So why was her mother bothering? She never did anything without a good reason.

Mrs Singh had her back to the path and did not know her daughter was there. Anji noticed the dejection in every line of her mother's body. Mrs Singh was on all fours, her head hanging down, 'like an old donkey's,' Anji thought. Then, rejected the idea as unworthy. But there was definitely something wrong.

'Mum!' she called. 'Mum?' She began to run towards her. 'Mum! What's wrong!'

She knelt beside Mrs Singh and put an arm around her mother's shoulders. A tear-stained face looked up into hers. Anji gasped. She had never seen her mother like this before. For a moment, she was lost for words. Then, instinctively, she hugged her and to her amazement, Mrs Singh buried her face in the girl's shoulder.

Genuinely alarmed now, Anji put both arms around her mother and held her tight. She heard Himal's voice calling, then he was stooping over them, asking what was wrong. Mrs Singh pushed Anji away and got to her feet. She made a pretence of smoothing her dress while she recovered her composure.

Himal gaped at them. 'What's happened, Mum? What are you doing the grass for?'

Mrs Singh turned away and began dabbing at her eyes with a small, lace handkerchief. Her mouth puckered and for a moment, Anji thought she was going to start crying again. She tried to hug her but Mrs Singh waved her away.

'Come inside,' she said in a wobbly voice. 'And I'll tell you the dreadful news.' Then she blew her nose very loudly.

A little later, Himal and Anji sat on the top step of the verandah talking in low voices. They could hear Mrs Singh moving about in the kitchen, getting supper ready.

'Poor old Dad,' said Himal.

Anji shook her head. 'Poor old both of them.'

'Well, it can't get any worse. Can it?' Himal asked.

17

Suresh and Hari were sitting in the shade of an old banyan tree, close to the long, bumpy track that joined them to the outside world. A mangy-looking dog walked towards them pursued by a small child waving a stick. The toddler put its hand on the animal's back and gurgled in delight. The dog moved away and the child sat down abruptly. It looked at the men in surprise then opened its mouth and yelled. A barefooted girl of about ten appeared and scooped it up. Suresh said something to her and she balanced the child on her hip and took it away.

The two men listened to the chatter of their families and shared the tail-end of a very thin cigarette. It had not been a good day. Three of the nests they had visited had been ravaged by wasps. One of them was still crawling with them when Hari reached it. He had been forced to flee in a hurry and one of his hands was raw from sliding down a patch of rough bark.

'We must try somewhere new tomorrow,' Suresh said. 'Or else we will have very little to take to the factory this week.'

Hari looked despondent. 'I have never known so many wasps before. They are like a plague.' He shook his head. 'For them to be here for one week, maybe two, is normal. But never for as long as this.' He sucked his hand. 'There are not many new places left to try and our children are getting hungry.'

'The wasps cannot last much longer,' Suresh assured him. 'They have to build their own nests soon and mate. You are too down-hearted.'

Hari picked up a stone and threw it aimlessly at a passing dragonfly. 'And you are too cheerful, Suresh. Just because your sister-in-law has left, you think everything is all right.'

Suresh was about to reply when they heard the sound of an approaching engine. They frowned at each other and scrambled to their feet. Vehicles of any sort were a rarity out here. A blue four-wheel drive came into sight with a plume of red dust trailing behind it. Its front wheels banged and jolted across a pothole. It braked and came to a sliding stop in front of them. Dogs barked hysterically and chickens ran panic-stricken while a dense cloud of dust rolled up and hid the vehicle.

Hari's wife ran out on to the track, seized a child by the arm and hustled it away. The rest of the family tried to hide behind her. The older girls peeked out from behind a ragged pink sheet that hung across the door of their shack.

Suresh gaped at Hari then wiped his hands on the seat of his trousers. They waited and watched the cloud of dust drift towards the banana trees. There was a radio playing inside the vehicle.

Whoever these people were, they were not from the Park, thought Hari, uneasily. There was no way they could have missed seeing all the no entry and warning signs. They had come here for a purpose. He scratched the back of his leg with his big toe and waited.

The doors of the vehicle were flung open and two men clambered out. They were not like any men Suresh and Hari knew. They were sleek and well fed and their clothes were clean and expensive-looking.

The taller of the two men took off his sunglasses and looked around. His nose wrinkled. He said something to his companion and they both laughed. He beckoned Hari and Suresh to come closer.

'You men the honey gatherers?'

Hari and Suresh glanced at each other then nodded shyly. The man put out his hand. Confused, Suresh took a step backwards.

The tall man laughed. 'Hey! I won't eat you. I'm here to welcome you.' And seeing their blank expressions, added, 'To the firm, of course.'

Shyly, without meeting his eyes, Suresh shook the stranger's hand. 'What firm's this?' he muttered to Hari.

But the stranger heard him and smiled broadly. He had a gold crown on one tooth.

'You can't have forgotten already!' He sounded thoroughly surprised. 'I thought my boss, Mr Sam, met you recently and told you what we're all going to be doing?'

Suresh and Hari looked at each other in surprise. 'Not recently, no,' said Hari.

'It was months ago,' Suresh put in. 'We rather thought he was joking.'

'Well he wasn't and that's why I'm here now,' the tall man enthused. 'So let me introduce myself. My name is Katni,' he told them. 'And I'm the manager in Amra. We've had some delays setting up, but we'll be opening very soon. And you're going to be my best workers. I know you are.'

The other man unwrapped a packet of chewing-gum and slid a piece into his mouth. He was shorter than Katni but much more powerfully built. One of his earlobes was missing. He joined Katni and stood beside him, chewing. He still wore his sunglasses.

'This is Pauli,' the manager smiled. 'He works with me.'

Hari held out his hand, then, embarrassed, let it drop. Pauli was not interested in shaking hands. Suresh looked away, pretending he hadn't noticed.

'How much do they pay you now for the honey?' Katni demanded.

They looked at each other again. 'Sixty rupees a kilo,' Suresh told him.

Hari listened in disbelief. That was twice the amount the factory gave them, even on a good day. But Katni did not seem in the least put out.

'I'll pay you a hundred. Just so long as the quality stays the same and you're reliable. And I'll need five kilos a week to start with. Perhaps more later.'

Hari pinched himself. He was trying to work out how much money that would mean. Suresh was talking freely now about all the other things they could bring in from the forest. Katni let him do so for a few moments then put up a hand to stop him.

'Sounds good!' He paused and lowered his voice. He spoke almost confidentially. 'Do you want to know what I pay the very best rates of all for?'

They waited to be told.

Katni grinned. 'Animal products,' he said, very deliberately.

'You mean, like peacock feathers?' Suresh suggested. There was something about his tone of voice that made Hari look at him in surprise.

Pauli took a clasp knife from his pocket. He pulled out a blade and began to clean his fingernails.

'Yes,' agreed Katni, nodding. 'Yes. They're useful. Always in great demand from our customers. Especially people in America.'

'Antlers,' yawned Pauli, without looking up. 'Sambar stags, blackbuck.'

'What about skins?' asked Suresh. Hari stared at him, perplexed.

Katni's smile widened. 'Well now, there's an interesting thought.'

'Perhaps you mean tiger skins?' Suresh said quietly. 'Or leopard?'

Katni spread his hands but said nothing.

Suresh swallowed So this was what these people were really after. He met Hari's gaze and looked away. There was a long silence.

'It's entirely up to you,' Katni said eventually. He waved his hand towards the watching women and children. 'I'll be happy to pay you for your honey. More than happy too. But if you think it would be good to provide your families with some well-deserved essentials . . .'

'How much?' Suresh demanded.

Katni considered. 'For a good skin, up to two thousand rupees.'

Hari's head swam. That was more than a month's wages. And a good one at that.

Suresh's voice sounded hoarse. 'How much for bones?'

'We can discuss all that later,' Katni said smoothly. 'Let's not rush things. You are free men. There is no pressure. It's up to you what you bring in.' He looked at Pauli. 'Do you want to say anything?'

Pauli snapped his knife shut. 'Everything we've discussed today is just between the four of us. Understand?' He made them look at him. 'No one else must know. We respect your privacy. But you say nothing to anyone. Remember that. And we'll all be happy!'

'Good!' Katni smiled. 'I'm glad we understand each other.' He pulled out a thick roll of money.

They watched in disbelief.

Slowly, deliberately, Katni counted off ten bank-notes. 'Five each,' he smiled. 'As a token of our esteem. An advance on all the money you're both going to make.' Then he pushed the money away in a trouser pocket.

'Next time!'

The two of them got back into the four-wheel drive. The radio boomed and they drove off.

The honey gatherers stood in a billowing cloud of dust.

'We will talk later,' Suresh told Hari, as their families ran towards them.

18

Inspector Singh had had enough of work. It had been the longest and worst day of his life. For the tenth time that afternoon, he looked at his watch. There was still another hour to go before work officially ended. But he didn't care any more. He just wanted to get out of these Headquarters and be by himself for a while.

The evening ahead was going to be awful. He had left Mrs Singh in floods of tears. And if he was totally honest, he didn't want to tell his children about his promotion. Or lack of it. Himal and Anji would outwardly sympathise but what if they secretly regarded him as a failure? Which he was, of course. Either way, he thought miserably, his standing with them was going to be diminished.

He put his head around the door of the clerk's office to say goodnight. Ambrose was standing by the fax machine. He looked up frowning, saw Inspector Singh, and went hot with embarrassment.

'It's for you,' he said. 'It's just come in.' Then added, 'Dowi, I'm really sorry.'

Inspector Singh stared at him. He had known Ambrose for close on eight years, yet in all that time, the clerk never used his first name while at work. What on earth was this all about? Full of premonition, he took the sheet of paper Ambrose handed him.

Himal and Anji sat at the supper table and listened in silence. They tried to avoid meeting each other's eyes and wished they were not there. Their father sat at one end of the table being very withdrawn. 'Just looking really miserable,' Anji thought.

'They are such fools in Delhi,' Mrs Singh was saying. 'Your father knows more about tigers than any one else in India.' She clattered their dishes into the sink. 'And if he was overlooked because he is not from university, let that be a lesson to both you children.'

'Good old Mum!' Himal thought. 'Tactful to the end!'

'Yes! That's the way the world is these days,' she added.

Inspector Singh looked up and said quietly, 'In that case, you'll be glad to hear that some things never change.' He paused while they all stared at him. 'We had a fax just before I left work. Seems like I'm going to have a new boss. A Superintendent Malik.'

'A Superintendent!' His wife's hand flew to her mouth. 'But that's terrible! Now there'll be no need for a Chief Inspector here as well. That's why you were passed over. That's the real reason!' She clicked her tongue and sighed, loudly.

'He's the nephew of the minister for health in the present government,' Inspector Singh told them and added drily, 'I suppose that must be a help. He's worked in Delhi all his life, on the staff. Now, it seems, he needs practical experience for his next promotion. And he's coming to us.'

'But that's so unfair!' Anji burst out.

'Is he married?' Mrs Singh demanded. 'How old is he?'

'When's he starting?' Himal asked.

Inspector Singh shook his head wearily. 'He's married and I'm told his wife is a Delhi society lady. So she won't be coming down here very much.'

Mrs Singh looked a shade less unhappy.

'He is young,' Inspector Singh went on. 'A real high-flyer by the sound of it.'

'When's he coming, Dad?' Himal insisted.

'In five days' time,' his father told him. 'And yes, Anji, life is unfair. But there's nothing any of us can do about that.'

'It's always been dog eats dog,' said Mrs Singh with a shake of her head.

'What a pity it can't be tiger eats dog,' said Himal.

Inspector Singh looked at him. 'That's rather illogical, Himal! But I think I know what you mean.' And he reached out his hand and ruffled Himal's hair.

19

'Hari! You are the worst type of pessimist,' Suresh shouted. 'Why must you always look on the dark side of everything!'

'And you, my friend, are as stupid as a sloth bear,' Hari retorted. 'And as greedy.'

The two men faced each other, their faces working in anger.

'I am not greedy for myself,' Suresh snapped. 'It is only for my wife and children. A man has a duty to look after his family.' He clutched at Hari's arm. 'And what would your wife say if I told her what you are intending to give up?'

Hari shook off his hand. 'You do that, Suresh, and I will kill you!'

Suresh was genuinely shocked. His mouth opened in surprise. He backed away and the words lay between them like a snake in both their paths.

'I'm sorry, Suresh! I'm sorry!' Hari exclaimed, banging his forehead with a fist. 'I did not mean that. Truly, I didn't.'

Suresh said nothing. He looked sorrowfully at the ground instead.

'You see what this man Katni is doing to us, already?' Hari cried out. 'He is a wicked man. He is a poacher. He will kill all the tigers if we let him.' He flung his arms wide. There were tears trickling down his face. 'That man we met in the marketplace. Mr Sam! You think he is a good man? Someone like you, who is only doing it to feed his family?' He broke off, visibly upset.

Suresh took a deep breath. His voice took on a soothing tone. 'Hari,' he said. 'Of course we're not going to kill tigers. They're our friends. They have as much right to live their lives as we do.'

'We're all part of the forest!' Hari shouted. 'It's their home. It's our home. We're all different but we belong here! No animal is more deserving than any other.'

Suresh nodded vigorously. 'You're so right, Hari. But don't forget. The tiger always leaves part of his kill for the jackals and the scavengers. All I'm asking is why can't we take those old tiger bones by the flat rock and sell them to get money for food and clothes?'

Hari waved his hands at him in impotent frustration. 'Because it is not honourable,' he spluttered.

'Just the bones, Hari?' Suresh pleaded. 'Just this once!'

Hari groaned out loud. He pulled up his old vest and wiped his eyes. His voice was muffled. 'All right. Just this once. But never again!'

20

The thing Kuma dreaded most was happening. There was a rogue male out there in the darkness. A rival to Raji, her mate and the sire of her cubs. A challenger for his territory and everything that went with it. Herself included. A male tiger, twice her size and certain death for the cubs, roared his challenge into the night. The whole forest listened and trembled at the ferocity of his roar.

The hair rose along her spine. This was no ordinary challenger. Or another young wanderer chancing his luck. She knew that instinctively. This one was different. Totally self-assured. His confidence seemed absolute. She waited with her ears pricked forward, listening impatiently for

Raji's roar of reply. But heard nothing. Alarmed, she bared her teeth at the darkness and wondered where he was.

On a night like this, the sound of the newcomer's roaring would carry for miles. Raji must be a long way away not to hear it. She licked her lips nervously as another coughing roar rolled towards her. This male was not that far distant. Behind her, one of the cubs sneezed.

Furious, she swung around. The cubs cringed and lowered their heads. The challenger was roaring again. She must get the cubs away from him. But where to go? The cave was now too small to use as a hiding place. Kuma thought quickly. This male tiger did not know the territory. He would soon need to find water. So she must keep clear of the big watering-holes. Kuma hissed at the cubs to follow and set off at a brisk trot in the opposite direction.

They spent the rest of the night in thick undergrowth close to the mouth of a deep ravine. It was a place she had often used in the past to hide the cubs, when they were small.

Dawn the next morning began like any other.

The sun rose in a great flaming ball, its shape distorted by the morning mist. The air smelt fresh and a heavy dew kept the dust down. Cobwebs glistened in the strengthening light. In the forest meadows, the chital herds lifted their muzzles to its warmth and tossed their heads in pleasure. Then remembered where they were and hurriedly scanned the tall grass for enemies.

This was an especially dangerous time for them. The monkeys were too busy either quarrelling with one another or stuffing themselves with fruit to pay much attention to what was happening on the ground. And this morning, not one of them spotted Kuma stalking the chital stag, until it was too late.

The tigress came racing out of nowhere and in a few smooth bounds sprang for the chital's neck. The stag crashed to the ground and thrashed ineffectively as Kuma suffocated it. The herd fled, their alarm calls loud in the early morning calm. Kuma got to her feet and stood panting over the body. Next, she stretched luxuriously. It was a good start to the day.

She grunted three times for the cubs to join her,

then, because she was hungry, she walked around to the animal's rump and settled down. Her teeth sliced through the skin and soon she was tearing off pieces of meat. She was surprised how long it was taking the cubs to appear. It was not like them.

Puzzled, she lifted her head. And stopped chewing. In an instant, she was on her feet, ears straining in disbelief. Next, she was running for dear life through the grass towards the cubs and their distress. She burst through the elephant grass, knowing what was waiting for her.

In the open ground beyond, Taza stood snarling at a huge tiger. Phur was a little way behind. Kuma did not hesitate. She sprang at the crouching male and landed full length across his back, her claws raking at the intruder's head, stretching for his eyes. For a split second, he lay rigid. Then she felt the shock and pain surging and twisting his body out from under her.

She hung on, trying to use her weight to hold him down. She raked his ribs with her back legs, wanting to rip through to the soft underbelly. But he was already standing, shrugging her off. She was slipping. She tried to bite down into his spine but he flung her to one side. His roaring filled her head. She could no longer think, conscious only of his massive strength. Then he was attacking her!

A massive paw hit her on the side of the head, knocking her off her feet. She was up like a flash, screaming at the cubs to run and hide. She leapt at his throat, biting, scratching, anything to distract him. She felt him flinch and saw blood streaming down his muzzle. His head battered at her chest, lifting her up, exposing her undersides. Steel-like claws slashed at her. She doubled up in agony.

She was fighting for breath, staggering under the shock of the blow, trying to suck air into her lungs. In a haze of pain she saw his jaws open very wide and knew he was coming in for the final killing bite. She rolled over on to her back like a cat in a last desperate defence. All four paws held close, claws bristling.

The big male slashed at her shoulder. Kuma rolled to meet the blow and ripped at his jaw. He dodged to one side, hesitated and turned away. Kuma scrambled up and crouched in the dust, snarling at him. Her tail lashed the ground in rage. He looked at her, roared again and, as if deciding that Kuma was not the tiger he needed to challenge, he turned and walked slowly away.

Kuma never took her eyes off him until she was sure he had gone. She began to lick her wounds. It was only then that the pain really started. The muscles in her shoulder were already stiffening. Blood oozed from a gash on her front leg. But it was her side and the long wounds along her ribs that made her gasp out loud.

She felt exhausted. All she wanted to do was to lie there and sleep. Instead, she dragged herself away. She needed water. Water to drink. Water to lie in and soothe her body. But she had to find the cubs. They could be anywhere. She was limping awkwardly, her shoulder increasingly painful. She put her full weight on the damaged leg and moaned. How long would it all take to heal? Until it did, there was no way she could hunt. They were all going to be hungry for many more days to come. She thought about the big male. He could return now at any time to kill the cubs and there was nothing she could do to stop him.

She plodded, head down, into the forest, hardly hearing the jeers from the monkeys. A pair of crows watched her from their perch in a tree. They flew down and screeched at her, flying dangerously close to her head. Kuma ignored them. Instead, she grunted for the cubs to come to her and headed for the stream.

21

There was only one boy at school whom Himal really disliked. His nickname was Babu. And he was in the same class. Inspector Singh had sacked Babu's father two years ago, for stealing. It was the second time he had been caught so the outcome was considered perfectly fair, by everyone else.

Ever since then, Babu did all he could to attack the Park. He and Himal were bitter enemies. The previous term, there had been a fight which ended in a draw. Although Babu was not as tall as Himal, he had broad shoulders and strong hands. Since then, the boys avoided each other and fed their mutual dislike by glowering and occasionally jostling each other, during games.

They had a new form master this term who thought it was time the feud ended. His name was Gupta and he was from Calcutta. It was the first time he had lived in rural India. He was a well-intentioned man, who believed that all misunderstandings could be cleared up if people only listened to the other person's point of view. Mrs Singh thought he was far too idealistic.

'Boys are strange creatures,' she declared. 'Best let them alone.'

Himal was not paying much attention when Mr Gupta came into the classroom. He was thinking instead about his father's gloomy prediction that in ten years' time, there would not be a single tiger left alive. He stared at the map of India on the wall and brooded.

Mr Gupta, meanwhile, was holding up a newspaper. 'There is a dreadful story in here,' he was saying. 'Apparently, poachers got into Delhi zoo overnight and killed a tiger. They cut it into pieces and even gouged out its eyes.' There was a murmur of disgust.

Himal was listening now, shocked out of his reverie. 'This is terrible!' he thought. 'A tiger killed in a zoo! A ZOO! Butchered like a helpless chicken! Dad must know more. I'll ask him as soon as he gets home!'

Mr Gupta was talking again. 'Now why would anyone do such a thing? Such a disgusting thing?'

Babu spoke first. 'To get money!'

Mr Gupta frowned. 'But to kill a helpless animal in a cage. Is that fair?'

'If you're very poor, what does it matter?' Babu demanded.

Himal's arm shot up. 'Sir!' he called. 'That's rubbish! That tiger was killed by a criminal gang. Its body parts will be on their way to Hong Kong by now.' He looked across the room at Babu. 'And it wasn't killed by any Robin Hood person, either! That's just stupid!'

Babu shouted something back Mr Gupta put up his hands and waved them all to silence.

'All right, Himal!' he called. 'Why don't you tell us what's really going on here?' He pointed to Babu. 'And you can say what you think, when he's finished.'

Himal thought quickly. What he said could

influence how his classmates felt about tigers for years to come. He must put his facts clearly. Start at the beginning. What was it his father had told him? He licked his lips.

'It's all to do with, "Traditional Chinese Medicine",' he said. 'It started a thousand years ago in China and now hundreds of millions of people all over the world believe that certain parts of a tiger's body can cure every disease. From malaria to toothache.'

Mr Gupta folded his arms and leant against his desk. He nodded encouragingly.

A girl called out, 'What do they use the eyes for?'

'To treat epilepsy,' Himal told her. 'And the teeth are supposed to cure fever.'

'What are the whiskers for?' someone else asked.

'Toothache,' he answered. And went on, 'But the bones are the important things. That's where the big money is. They grind the bones into powder and use it to make pills and lotions and oils and ointments.'

He thought for a moment. 'People think they can cure hundreds of things. You name it! Leprosy, heart attacks, muscle pain, liver disease, dog bites, rabies . . . Anything you can think of. And the demand just keeps on growing.'

Mr Gupta looked at him appraisingly. 'And more and more tigers are being killed to meet this demand.'

Himal nodded. 'Yes, Sir.'

'Do they make traditional medicine in this country?'

Himal shook his head. 'No! It's illegal in India and most of the rest of the world. It's all made in Hong Kong or mainland China. And in Korea and Taiwan too. It's a huge business. It's worth billions of dollars a year.'

'So it's organised crime, then?' Mr Gupta said. 'And what's a tiger worth to these people?'

Himal took a deep breath. 'By the time it gets to China, it could be well over ten thousand American dollars.'

Mr Gupta puffed out his cheeks in surprise.

'My father says the really big traffickers are based in cities like Delhi or Calcutta,' Himal went on. 'Their job is to get the bones and body parts out of India. They bribe the border guards and they've got politicians, lawyers and policemen on their payroll. It's very well organised.'

Babu said something and the boys next to him laughed.

'Who does the killing?' someone at the back wanted to know. 'Is it the same criminals?'

Himal felt his confidence grow. 'There's a huge network all across the country. The big crooks have people working for them all the way down to village level. That's where they recruit the men who set the traps or leave out the poisoned meat. The actual poachers. They pick small farmers or forest workers, mostly.' He looked over at Babu. 'And petty thieves.'

'How much do they get paid?' Mr Gupta asked

Himal shook his head. 'It's pathetic! They get twenty American dollars a tiger.'

'And that same carcass fetches ten thousand dollars in China? That's wicked!' Mr Gupta stated.

'Are there any poachers here in Amra?' a girl questioned.

Himal shrugged. 'There used to be until my father got rid of them.'

'Now, Babu,' Mr Gupta said, 'what do you say to all that? Do you agree with Himal?'

Babu scowled around. 'Himal's better at words than me,' he began.

Mr Gupta made soothing noises.

Babu shrugged. 'It's all right for Himal,' he told the schoolmaster. 'His father's got lots of money. But if you're poor like us, it's different.'

Himal started to protest but Mr Gupta ignored him. 'Go on!' he said.

Babu looked around at his friends. 'That tiger park where his father works is really big,' he began. 'Thousands of people can live there and grow crops. But they're not allowed to.' He frowned. 'The Park people throw you out if they find you there. People like me and my family starve so that tigers can live. It's unfair!'

The rest of the class were starting to argue amongst themselves.

Encouraged, Babu's voice grew louder. 'Himal goes on about these big criminals and how much money they make. And how the local people get hardly anything.' He turned and jabbed a finger at Himal. 'Well, take it from me, if you're very poor, twenty dollars is a heck of a lot of money. I'd do it for that! And I know a lot of others who'd do it too!'

A hubbub of cheers and booing broke out. Above all the noise, the school bell sounded for the end of the period. Mr Gupta tried to regain order then threw his hands in the air. He was glad to move on to his next class.

Himal told Anji what had happened during the bus ride home. 'You must tell Dad what he said,' was her immediate reaction.

'Babu's just full of it,' Himal told her. 'He said it just to sound big.'

'Even so, he might know more than you think,' she told him, looking serious. 'And if you won't tell Dad, then I will!'

22

The Superintendent arrived at noon. He drove through the main gate of the Park in a bright red Range Rover. Joshi saw him go past the stores and gaped. He did a quick mental calculation then snatched up the phone. 'He's here!' he warned. 'And his car's worth a fortune!'

The Range Rover stopped outside Park Headquarters. Inspector Singh came down the steps, buckling on his belt. A tall, hawk-faced man climbed out and looked around him. He was immaculately dressed in cream-coloured chinos and a blue silk shirt. On his feet, he wore tan loafers.

With tassels on, Inspector Singh noted as he

hurried down to greet him. 'Welcome to Kanla,' he smiled and sketched a salute.

The other man's expression did not change. 'And who are you?' he asked.

Inspector Singh introduced himself.

'And where are all the other departmental heads?' the Superintendent asked.

'At their posts. The elephant stables, the stores—'

'You got my signal yesterday?' the man interrupted.

Inspector Singh nodded.

'And I told you I would be here at twelve noon?'

Inspector Singh nodded again.

'I thought I asked you to have them all here to meet me?'

Inspector Singh felt his mouth go dry. 'Well,' he hesitated. 'I mean, what with the roads being so bad, I thought, we thought, you could be here at any time.'

Superintendent Malik frowned. 'I stayed at a cousin's place nearby. I did that deliberately, so as not to be late. One thing you'd better learn here and now, Singh, is that when I say a thing, I mean every last word.' He looked at his watch. 'I'll inspect my own quarters first and then my office. So have the others meet me there in thirty minutes' time. Oh! And my bags will need taking over.'

Inspector Singh's mouth opened and shut. 'Yes, Sir,' was all he could trust himself to say.

23

Dev Patel squatted down and hauled the elephant's foot on to his knee. He shifted round a couple of times to get comfortable then began to examine the wound. Fuja's trunk snaked over his shoulder and fingered the pocket of his shirt, searching for sugar lumps.

'What happened to her?' asked Himal.

It was Saturday but this time Anji was not with him. Under protest, she had been taken shopping by Mrs Singh to buy new shoes.

'It's a big scar, isn't it?' he added.

Dev nodded and pushed Fuja's trunk away. Her mahout slapped her with his hand and made angry noises. Fuja tossed her head then blew warm air over them.

'She's young and very playful,' the mahout told Himal. 'That's why she hurt her foot.'

'She was helping drag out an old tree stump,' Dev added. 'Only she got bored and wanted to do something else instead. That's how she backed into a really big root.'

'It was like iron,' the mahout explained. 'With a sharp edge.' He ran his finger along the scar. 'The vet had to come out from Headquarters. Fuja was very upset.'

Himal looked up at the elephant towering above them. 'How did you calm her down?'

'There was an older elephant there,' Dev said. 'She helped. Then we hobbled this one by the front legs and padlocked the chain to a tree.'

The mahout chuckled. 'She is a greedy one, this Fuja. She will do anything for mangoes. So we bribed her while the vet cleaned the wound. After that, we smeared ointment over it to keep out the infection.'

Dev straightened up. 'It's healed well,' he told the mahout. 'But I'm going to take her out for an hour or so. Then we'll see if she's fit enough to start work tomorrow.' He slipped two sugar lumps into his hand and held them out. The tip of Fuja's trunk tickled his neck as she thanked him.

Dev looked at the mahout. 'Mind if I take young Himal here with me? Only he might learn something.'

The mahout grinned. 'So long as he helps brush her down afterwards!'

'Fair enough?' asked Dev.

'Absolutely!' Himal nodded enthusiastically.

Fuja lifted her front leg to make a step and Dev climbed up. He sat on her head then looked down at Himal. 'Your turn,' he called. 'Here! Grab my hand.'

'Hang on to me if it gets bumpy,' he told Himal when the boy was settled behind him.

Dev tapped the side of the elephant's face with a long switch, squeezed Fuja behind the ears and they moved off. They left the stables at a slow walk and made their way past the mahouts' quarters. They went through the bustle of the little market and out on to a well-worn track. Within a minute, all sight and sound of the village had faded and they were in dense forest.

Himal stared into the impenetrable shadows on either side of the path and wondered how many unseen eyes were staring back. The forest was very still. There were no bird calls, no chattering monkeys, not even the hum of insects. And although it was the hottest part of the day, Himal shivered.

It was the first time he had realised how precarious human existence was. One moment, there had been hundreds of people all around him, laughing and shouting as they went about their daily business. The next, there were none. The village had been swallowed up in the immensity of nature. It might never have existed. The thought depressed him.

Fuja, however, was in fine humour and glad to be back out in the forest. Her wound had kept her off work for a week. She trumpeted with pleasure and tried to blow a trunkful of dust over them. Dev rapped her smartly with his switch and she settled down to break off leafy branches from the passing trees.

Dev leant over and peered back at Fuja's damaged foot, trying to gauge how much weight the elephant was actually putting on it.

'What are you looking for?' Himal asked.

'If her foot's properly mended,' Dev told him, 'she'll put it flat down on the ground. But if she hesitates or tries to walk on one side of it, she'll still need attention. Tell me if you see anything.'

By the end of the first mile, Fuja seemed to be walking normally with no obvious discomfort or stiffness. As they swayed along, Himal thought of Anji trying on shoes in a crowded Amra shop and of their mother, fussing over her. He smiled. She'd be so jealous when she heard about this. He bent down and studied Fuja's back foot again. Dev was saying something.

'I think she's fine. Can't see any discomfort. Can you?'

Himal shook his head. 'No. Nothing.'

'You in a great hurry to get back?' Dev asked. He looked round at Himal's face and laughed. 'There's a stream a couple of miles from here. She can drink there. Then we'll come back. Remind me,' he called over his shoulder, 'to show you something when we get there.'

Half an hour later, the forest began to open up. The trees shrank back and small clearings started to appear. A herd of deer watched them with mild curiosity. Fuja suddenly trumpeted.

'She can smell water,' Dev called. 'Look! There's the stream. Keep an eye out for tiger tracks,' he added. 'This is a good place for them. That female I told you about. The one with the cubs. Remember? This is her territory.'

They halted at the stream. Fuja sucked up a trunkful of water and poured it into her mouth. When she had had enough, Dev let her play. They sat there patiently while she turned over the smooth black pebbles on the bed of the stream. She handed one up to Dev and blew water over his arm and chest as he took it from her.

'No fresh pugmarks,' he said, looking around.

'You told me to remind you of something.'

'That's right,' Dev nodded. 'I will. Hang on tight for a moment!'

He uttered a ferocious-sounding oath and urged Fuja up the far bank. Fuja lurched and Himal slipped to one side.

Dev thrust an arm back and gripped the boy. 'Use your knees!' he shouted. 'Grip tight with them!'

Himal did so and pulled himself upright.

They reached the top of the bank without any further problem. 'It's steeper than it looks,' Dev called, reassuringly. 'But it'll be all right now.' A little later he asked, 'Has your father ever told you about elephants and death?'

Himal frowned. 'No. I don't think so.'

'There's a tiger skeleton near here,' Dev said. 'It's been there for some time. You can't see it because the grass has grown. But Fuja will find it. You wait and see.'

'How do you know?' Himal asked.

'Death fascinates them,' Dev replied. 'Every elephant I bring here does the same thing. They stoop over the bones. They pick them up and turn them over and then they put them back in exactly the same place. Very respectful. And that's strange. You know how they hate tigers?'

Himal nodded.

'And I'll tell you something else,' Dev went on. 'Sometimes, on patrol, we find elephant bones. Now that really gets them. They start trumpeting and throwing dust in the air. I once saw them covering a freshly killed body with branches.'

'To keep tigers off?' Himal suggested.

'Could be but I think there's a lot more to it. They really get distressed. Just like humans. They make humming noises as if they're singing. It's very strange.'

Himal saw they were approaching a wide, flat rock.

'Not far now. It's on the other side,' Dev said. 'Just watch Fuja.'

They crossed the rock and lumbered on. Dev gave a cry of surprise. He stood up and looked back then turned Fuja around. He shot a glance at Himal.

'This is the place. I've been here a dozen times.'

Minutes later, he halted the elephant and dismounted. He bent double and scanned the ground.

'This is the place! I know it is.'

'Fuja doesn't seem very bothered,' Himal put in.

The elephant was browsing on a nearby bush.

Dev shook his head. 'It doesn't make sense. I know the bones were here. I've touched them. The skull. Bits of backbone. But it's all gone. There's nothing. Not even splinters.'

'Perhaps a hyena ate them,' Himal suggested.

Dev shook his head. 'Unlikely after all this time. Not when there's so many better pickings around.'

Silently, he remounted and turned Fuja for home. 'That's a mystery!' he said. 'A real mystery.'

His mobile phone rang. Dev grabbed at his shirt pocket and fumbled to undo the button. 'Hello?' he said.

Himal listened to the growing excitement in his voice.

'I've got Himal here with me—' He broke off. Then, 'So I bring him with me?' He swivelled round and looked at the boy. 'OK. We'll be there in an hour. And listen, Dowi. Be very careful. Don't take any chances.'

He thrust the mobile back in his pocket. 'A patrol's found an injured tiger. Your father and the vet are going out to it. So are we! You just do exactly what I tell you and there'll be nothing to worry about. Hold tight!'

24

'There they are!' cried Dev, flinging out an arm. 'Down by those bushes.' He tapped Fuja smartly with his switch. Her head swung round and they crashed through the thorn scrub beside the trail.

Himal stared over Dev's shoulder and gasped. A tiger lay stretched on the ground a hundred metres away. As he watched, she raised her head and tried to get up. Beyond her, two large cubs crouched, ears flat against their skulls, snarling. There were three elephants standing in an uneasy line, in front of them. Himal recognised his father immediately, and the vet.

Inspector Singh looked across at them and cupped his hands. 'Stop! Hold it there!' he called. 'Dev, wait! I want this done as calmly as possible.'

Obediently, Dev brought Fuja to a halt.

'We're going to tranquillise the mother,' Inspector Singh called. 'Circle round and come up beside me.'

'This could be exciting,' Dev called back to Himal. 'Keep an eye on those cubs!'

Even as he said it, the bigger cub got to its feet and began to roar.

'Careful!' Dev warned, talking more to himself than Himal.

The cub was moving forward towards the waiting elephants.

'Watch out!' Dev shouted. 'Tiger!'

The cub was racing towards Inspector Singh's elephant. Three final strides and it sprang at the elephant's head. The elephant screamed and reared up. The mahout was thrown backwards. Himal shouted. For a terrible moment, he thought both men were going to fall off. He was aware of Dev yelling like a madman and almost lost his own balance as Fuja lurched forward at a run.

The cub was back on the ground. It was difficult

to see in all the dust. Everyone was shouting; the elephants trumpeting in rage. From the corner of his eye, Himal saw his father pulling the mahout upright. But by then, the vet's elephant was charging the cub. Himal saw its tusks sweeping down to impale the tiger. In the nick of time, the cub slipped to one side, slashed at the elephant's cheek, then leapt out of the way. It twisted round in midair and landed in a crouching position facing them. The other cub ran to meet it, roaring furiously. For a moment, both cubs snarled defiance. Then they bounded away.

'This is going to be fun!' Dev cried, as they joined the others. 'Glad I'm not a vet!'

It took Inspector Singh some minutes to calm his elephant and bring it under control. Finally, she stood breathing noisily, waving her trunk up and down. The vet was already at work. There were claw marks high up on the elephant's leg. Two thin streams of blood trickled down. The vet worked quickly, giving the wounds a final swab of disinfectant.

'That'll do for the time being,' he said. He was an Australian and an old friend of Himal's.

Dev dismounted and joined him. He took the elephant's trunk in his arms and hugged it. He talked to it in a low voice then gave it a friendly slap.

'She'll be OK,' he told Inspector Singh. 'A bit shaken but nothing a good warm feed won't cure.'

Inspector Singh looked at his son and gave him a questioning smile. 'You all right?'

Himal nodded enthusiastically. He was too excited to say anything. His heart was pounding. It was all fantastic. Anji would never forgive him. A wide smile spread across his face.

The vet grinned up at Himal and shook his head.

'I must be getting really old,' he said, 'if the mahouts are getting as young as you!'

'Let's get started!' Inspector Singh ordered.

The vet waved a hand in acknowledgement and bent over a long canvas bag. He drew out a dart gun, loaded it and snapped the breech shut. He pulled the butt of the gun into his shoulder and concentrated on the sick tigress. There was a sharp hiss of compressed air and the next instant a bright blue dart was embedded in Kuma's side. She jerked upright, tried to pull it out with her teeth and fell back.

'How long before it takes?' Dev asked.

'Three minutes,' the vet called back. 'Then she'll be out for the count.'

'You stay up there with Dev,' Inspector Singh called to Himal. 'But keep your eyes wide open and shout if those cubs return!'

The vet studied his watch. 'Time to go,' he called and picked up his medical bag.

Warily, they approached the tigress and carefully knelt beside her. 'She's out cold,' the vet said with the slightest touch of relief in his voice. Kuma's large round eyes stared up at the sky. They could see the clouds reflected in them. It was an odd sensation.

'Been in a fight,' said the vet, shaking his head. 'Come off worse too, by the look of it.'

Inspector Singh nodded. 'There's been a new male about. The children have heard him roaring. We were talking about it at supper recently.' He stroked Kuma's ears. 'They make such wonderful mothers, tigers. I think he's done this to her.'

The vet sucked his teeth. 'This shoulder wound

is really bad. Deep too.' He made a face, opened his bag and brought out a long syringe. 'We'll give her this for starters.' He flicked the side of the needle and watched liquid spray out.

'A mega shot of antibiotics. If this doesn't work, nothing will.'

He took hold of a pinch of Kuma's skin and watched the colourless liquid empty into her. 'Right! Let's get her cleaned up.'

He worked in silence; swabbing, cleansing and shaving the fur on either side of the gash to make a bald patch. When he was finished, he selected a needle and closed the wound with ten neat stitches. Finally, he smeared ointment over it.

'She won't like the taste of that,' he grunted. 'OK. Let's turn her over.'

It took the two of them all their strength and Inspector Singh winced when he saw the long claw marks along Kuma's side. He ran his fingers along them.

'She was lucky he didn't disembowel her,' he told them. 'A couple of centimetres lower and she'd be dead.'

The vet was rummaging in his bag. He stood up

and called, 'Dev! Can you bring me my other bag please? The small one. I need more drugs.'

'Just sit still,' Dev told Himal. 'I'll be back in a moment.'

Dev found the bag and took it over. The vet set to work cleaning out the pus and dried blood. When he had finished, he sat back on his heels and looked at them. 'You know something?'

Dev shook his head. 'Not too much,' and he laughed.

The vet sniffed. 'It's not so much the physical damage that kills them,' he said. 'I mean, tigers are pretty tough animals.' He wiped his nose on the back of his hand. 'No! It's all the bacteria they carry round on their teeth and claws. That's what gets them. Most of the time they die of blood-poisoning.'

Inspector Singh nodded in agreement and patted Kuma's head. 'So, is this one going to be all right?'

The vet made a tilting motion with his hand. 'Wouldn't like to say. She's got a chance. But that's about all.'

Himal meanwhile stared at the tiger. It was the

nearest he had ever been to one. If only he had brought his camera. She was the most beautiful thing he had ever seen. He wondered if they would let him touch her fur. Or even her teeth! He licked his lips. He didn't want to be a nuisance but surely they couldn't say no.

He took a deep breath, looked around and saw the big cub. It was about forty metres away to the rear of his father and the others. As Himal watched, it ran forward and crouched down by an ant-hill. There was no possible doubt. The cub was stalking them!

He gasped in horror. This was real and there was no time to waste. He pushed himself up on to Fuja's head and shouted, 'Dad! The cub! It's behind you!'

The mahouts heard him and turned to see where he was pointing. One of them began to shout. His elephant trumpeted and stamped its feet. Himal saw his father stand up and look around.

One of Kuma's back paws twitched. A shudder ran through her. She opened her jaws. 'Time to go,' warned the vet, snapping shut his bag.

The elephants were on the move and starting to surge to and fro. Clouds of dust were rising. The vet ran towards his elephant. The mahout saw him coming and wheeled to meet him. The elephant passed within touching distance of Dev and Inspector Singh who leapt back in alarm. Thick red dust swirled around them.

'I can't see a damn thing,' Inspector Singh cried. He peered round, looking for Dev. The next moment, he realised the vet's elephant was backing towards him 'Watch out!' he shouted and flung himself to one side. He cursed loudly. Then shouted at the mahout.

He could feel the ground shaking. The elephants were huge grey shapes looming in and out of the confusion. He was in real danger of being trampled. And then, the dust shifted and he saw the cub! The big one. Crouching, twenty metres away. Its head swinging towards him. He waited for the exact moment when their eyes should meet. He even fancied he saw them widen in comprehension when they did.

Dev must have remounted. He hoped to God he had. The cub was running towards him, belly close to the ground, shoulders held high. The classic attack posture of the tiger. Where was his own elephant! For Heaven's sake! He was rooted to the spot. His legs had turned to water. He was in a strange new world where there was no sound or fury. There was just himself and this young tiger. And there was nothing he could do about it. It was fate.

The cub was in the open now. There was no longer any need to stay in cover. The man could not get away. It sank lower to the ground. Measuring the distance.

Himal saw the cub run forward and knew instinctively that it was about to attack. He couldn't see who or what it was after, but that didn't matter. He flung himself forward. Then he was sitting up on Fuja's head and squeezing his legs together.

Obediently, the elephant moved forward. He thrust his right leg against her cheek and pushed as hard as he could. She turned in the same direction. He banged his knees behind her ears and she broke into a trot. He kept on doing it and she began to run.

The cub was directly in front of Himal. Unaware of him. Bunching itself up for the final explosive leap. Someone nearby was screaming. A long high-pitched wail of terror. The hairs on Himal's neck lifted. Fuja was pounding towards the tiger. Ten metres now . . . coming nearer . . . And then, briefly, he saw his father! He was standing motionless. He was the prey!

Fuja screamed at it. The cub snatched a look behind. Its mouth opened in shock. As it tried to leap out of the way, a long, muscular trunk came swinging down and knocked it off its feet. The cub rolled completely over and fled from the shouting, stamping, whooping scrum of men and elephants, to the safety of the forest.

There were elephants crowding in on either side. Fuja came to a stop. A mahout stepped across from another elephant and slid down in front of the boy. Himal saw Dev limping badly and hanging on to the vet's arm. He was waving at him and shouting something. And there was his father, waiting for him.

In a daze, he got down from Fuja. His father took him by the shoulders and stared at him.

There were tears in his eyes. His whole body was shaking. Then they were hugging each other, fiercely. 'Thank you, my son!' whispered Inspector Singh. 'Thank you!'

25

'My son is a hero!' exclaimed Mrs Singh, beaming at Himal.

Himal shifted his feet. He was becoming tired of his mother's constant praise.

'Mum!' he chided for what seemed the umpteenth time. 'It wasn't like that at all. It was an accident. I didn't even know it was Dad. It just sort of happened.'

'And so modest too,' Mrs Singh enthused, ignoring him.

Himal looked at Anji and shrugged. 'It just happened. That's all. I didn't mean to do anything.'

Mrs Singh laughed. 'You must not be too

modest, Himal. In this life it is no bad thing to be regarded as brave. It helps you get on.'

'It was brave. Whatever you say, Himal,' agreed Anji. 'Very brave.' She turned to her mother and frowned. 'Mum! You're embarrassing Himal. Please don't go on any more.'

'I am going to make Himal his favourite supper,' Mrs Singh told them. 'Why don't you both go outside and greet your father when he comes home.'

They sat on the top step of the verandah watching the sun slide down the sky. It would be pitch dark in half an hour.

'How did it really feel?' Anji asked. 'Were you terrified?'

Himal shook his head. 'It all happened so fast,' he replied. 'I don't think I felt anything. Well, not until I saw Dad standing there. Then I was terrified.'

'Well, I think it was brilliant,' she told him. 'And I'm as sick as a dog I wasn't there too. Why do all the exciting things happen to you?'

Himal considered. 'I don't know about exciting,' he said slowly. 'But here's something odd. Dev called it a mystery.'

And he told her about the bones.

Anji made him repeat the story. 'But it's obvious!' she cried when he had finished. 'If it wasn't animals who took the bones then it's got to be people. Now why should anyone want to take away a lot of old tiger bones?'

They stared at each other and their eyes widened.

'You mean poachers?' Himal asked.

Anji nodded. 'Who else would?'

'Himal! It's time you put up the mosquito screens,' Mrs Singh called. 'Then come and see what I'm making for you!'

Anji put a hand on Himal's arm. 'We'd better tell Dad. But not tonight. He's had a tough day. Agreed?'

Himal nodded. 'Tomorrow, then.'

'There can't be any other reason, can there?' Anji asked. 'Something we've not thought of.'

'Let's see what Dad thinks,' Himal told her. 'Tomorrow.'

26

Kuma opened her eyes. She lay staring up at a grey sky and tried to remember where she was. She sat up and yelped in sudden pain. Her side ached. She bent to lick it and saw the claw marks. Then she remembered. The fight! What had happened to the cubs?

She got to her feet and stood there groaning as the blood returned to cramped muscles. She limped forward and felt almost unsteady at first. She looked around and to her great relief saw the cubs squatting down, some distance away. They had their backs to her and appeared to be eating. She began to trot towards them. Then, as her body relaxed, she started to run. She called them and saw them look towards her.

The cubs threw themselves at her, growling in pleasure. They rubbed heads and nipped each other's ears and butted each other's chest and sides, until Kuma yowled in protest. She licked their faces and seized their necks in her mouth and gently shook them. Taza locked jaws with her and wrestled for advantage.

Kuma tasted blood on his jaws and snarled as the pangs of her own hunger flared up. The cubs had already gorged themselves on the chital carcass the men had thrown to them, earlier. Kuma ate for the next hour, devouring everything except for the skull and four small hooves.

In the distance, thunder boomed. Kuma looked up in surprise and only then realised how much the light had faded. A vast blue-black cloud covered half the sky. Forked lightning flashed across its face.

A cold wind had begun to blow. It gathered up the dead leaves and flung them in their faces. It battered the elephant grass, alternately flattening it then tossing it high into the air, trying to tear it out by the roots. The growing menace of thunder rumbled ever closer towards them. There was a sharp pitter-pat of rain. Tiny clouds of dust kicked up in front of them. Then, with a roar, the storm engulfed them.

Soon the ground was running with water. It filled every hole, every depression in the ground, and went swirling off in a bubbling flood. Lightning crackled, dangerously close, and the air smelt of burning. Hailstones the size of plum stones came whipping down, shredding leaves and ripping off the smaller branches. The tigers hung their heads and waited patiently for its lash to ease.

Kuma knew that when the storm was over, the forest floor would be littered with dead peacocks and pigeons, waiting to be eaten. But the new male challenger was also in there somewhere. The rain would have washed away most animal scent markings. So now she would have even less chance of knowing where he might be. The chances of their running into him again were now much worse.

27

'Come on in, Dev,' called Inspector Singh, sympathetically.

Dev propped his stick against the desk and lowered himself into a chair. He grimaced as he did so. His bare foot and ankle were tightly bandaged.

'How are you feeling?' Inspector Singh asked. 'That's a nasty sprain, I hear.'

'I'll be walking on it in a week,' Dev said. Then looked embarrassed. 'I think I fell over the tiger, if you can believe it!'

Inspector Singh smiled. 'Well just don't go making a habit of it. You mightn't be so lucky next time.'

Dev shook his head. 'We were both lucky. When

I think what could have happened out there! Your boy did well!'

'He saved my life,' Inspector Singh said with pride. 'His mother wants me to put him forward for a bravery medal! She's writing to the head teacher as well.'

They smiled at each other, remembering the confusion and what might have been.

'Any news of the tiger?' Dev asked. 'Is she still alive?'

Inspector Singh nodded. 'She was earlier this morning. And the cubs were there too. With a bit of luck she'll have fed by now.'

'I'll have some more meat dropped off this afternoon,' Dev suggested.

Inspector Singh hesitated then said quietly, 'What's all this about some old tiger bones disappearing? The children told me about them at breakfast.'

Dev sucked his teeth. 'I meant to tell you before but what with all the carry-on, it went clean out of my head.'

'Tell me now,' the Inspector reassured, and listened in silence.

'You're saying there was absolutely nothing left?' he asked when Dev had finished.

'Not even a splinter. I double-checked.'

'When were you last there? Before this time, I mean.'

Dev frowned. 'Ten days ago. I took a patrol out to talk to the honey gatherers. I wanted to see what they knew about this new male tiger.'

'And the bones were there?'

Dev nodded. 'Yes. I saw them.'

Inspector Singh picked up a pencil and began tapping it on the desk top. 'I wonder if Suresh or Hari have seen anything strange going on.'

'You think it's poachers, don't you?'

Inspector Singh looked troubled. 'I can't think of any other explanation. Can you?'

A gloomy silence fell between them.

'I think I'll take a look myself. And talk to them. By the way, what did they know about this new male?'

Dev made a face. 'Nothing much. I was surprised.' Then he looked at the Inspector and smiled. 'Can I make a suggestion? Take Anji with you when you go. I can occupy Himal with something else. She'd love it.'

Inspector Singh considered. 'It's a public holiday tomorrow. I'll do it then.'

28

Mr Sam stood at the open door of his carriage and looked with distaste at the jostling crowd on the platform. Many of them carried their possessions on their heads, wrapped up in old white sheets. Others were struggling with bursting suitcases, often held together with string. As the doors of the train opened, people on the platform surged forward, eager to find a place on board. At the same time, the passengers on the train were themselves crowding out. The two waves met with something of a shock. Mr Sam knew that for the next five minutes, the platform would be full of people trying to barge their way through. It was ridiculous.

He sighed. He was lucky to be so tall and well built. On occasions like these, he felt like an ocean liner breasting through an armada of fishing skiffs. There were easier ways for him to travel, of course. By air, for one. With a taxi waiting at the other end. But in Mr Sam's experience, airline tickets were too easily traced. Going by train, while often exhausting, was very discreet. No one knew who you were, where you were going, or how long you stayed when you got there.

He emerged from the station and stood in the swirling noise and bustle of Amra. Taxi-drivers shouted for his custom. A beggar with no legs was dragging himself towards him. The heat hit him like a hot sponge. He swore out loud. He hated these small towns. Not a building in this wretched place was air-conditioned. The hotels were just glorified dosshouses full of cockroaches. He turned on his heel and ignored the beggar's outstretched hand.

Last night, he had been three hundred kilometres away in the state capital, meeting some very influential men. A deal had been agreed for the safe transit of some of his most 'special' products. It had been a very constructive meeting and held in an American-style hotel complete with indoor fountains and an ice-making machine on every floor.

He sighed at the memory, then banished the thought from his mind. This sort of inconvenience went with the territory. It would be the same until the day came when he could afford to retire. Right now, that was still a couple of years away. Longer, if things stayed as they were. The last monsoon had been particularly bad for business.

It had rained solidly for three months. Roads, bridges and railway lines had all been washed away. Many of them still needed repair. Luckily, the main line north had been restored and some trains were running. His cash flow had all but dried up and the bank was becoming impatient. It was all so unreasonable when good customers in Hong Kong were screaming at him for more product. A complete tiger carcass was now fetching up to fifty thousand American dollars. But he couldn't tell the bank that.

Grimly, he set out to walk the couple of hundred metres to the storehouse. Katni, the

Amra manager, had at long last opened it, after a lot of money had changed hands behind the scenes. He thought about tiger traps and the consignment he had recently bought. That had been a bargain. The best steel-jaw traps in the world and he had bought them for nine dollars each. They should be here any day. He reached the storehouse and knocked. Katni had better be in. It was time to rattle his cage.

29

'Look! Tiger tracks!' Inspector Singh called. 'Fresh ones, too.'

Anji craned her neck. 'Where, Dad?'

Inspector Singh pulled their elephant off to one side and pointed. 'In the sand by the stream. See them?'

Anji looked and gasped. A perfect set of pugmarks led down to the water's edge and up the sandy bank on the other side.

'How recent are they?' she asked.

Her father moved the elephant closer. 'Very recent, I'd say. Take a look. The tracks are only half filled with water.' He looked around and spotted the patch of crushed grass. 'That's where it was lying just before we came along.'

The elephant gave a low rumble and raised her trunk.

'She's scenting,' Inspector Singh said. 'Trying to see where the tiger's got to. Hang on tight and we'll cross the stream.'

At the top of the bank, they paused. The elephant trumpeted and stamped a foot. The rumble grew louder.

'Keep your eyes peeled!' Inspector Singh warned, and started to back away. 'That tiger must be very close.'

Anji peered into the deep shadows under the trees. The elephant trumpeted again and Anji heard her father gasp. She looked over his shoulder and there, ten metres away, stood the largest tiger she had ever seen. It came out of the darkness and stood looking at them.

Anji stared in wonder at the size and beauty of the animal. Its eyes were the colour of old gold. Its head was a living mask of white and black and orange stripes. She was suddenly sure the tiger was looking directly at her. She stared back, trying not to blink. And as she did so, she concentrated all her feelings of awe and respect into her gaze. Would the tiger understand?

The tiger snarled and the dagger-like teeth gleamed. The elephant shifted uneasily. Her father was talking to it and Anji was suddenly afraid. What if the tiger turned on them? It would only take a moment for the tiger to reach up and pluck them off the elephant's back, like so much ripe fruit. The elephant took another step backwards.

The tiger's tongue lolled out of its mouth and it stood panting. Its head drooped and it walked slowly back into the cool of the shadows.

Inspector Singh let out a long breath. 'That was the biggest male I've seen in years.' His voice was thick with admiration. He looked around at Anji and smiled. 'What do you think about that? Wasn't he beautiful?' He chuckled. 'Your brother is going to be very jealous.'

He started talking to the elephant again. She was still rumbling with displeasure. 'She's angry with me,' he called over his shoulder. 'She doesn't approve of tigers one little bit.' He bent over and slapped her trunk. 'We'd better find her some bananas to say sorry. Hang on, now.'

Minutes later, they reached the flat rock. They dismounted and Anji kept close to her father while he walked up and down, searching for any sign of the bones.

'Looks as if Dev was right,' he said at last. 'There's not a trace.'

'Now what?' she asked.

Inspector Singh looked at his watch. 'Time to go and see the honey men. They'll know if anyone does.'

They went at a steady pace for the next hour. At first, they crossed wide expanses of elephant grass. In places it was tall enough to brush Anji's ankles.

'Old buffaloes often hide up in here,' Inspector Singh told her. 'It's good cover from the dog packs.'

They trotted in and out of tall stands of trees where the air was cool and smelt of dead leaves. At other times, they squinted into the glare of the plains and kept a lookout for the huge ant-hills that loomed up out of the heat haze. Anji was aware for the first time of the sheer size of it all. She imagined being lost out here. She also wondered what unseen eyes might be watching them, and looked behind, unable to resist a shiver. The only signs of movement in these vast open spaces were the dust-devils that careered across the baking earth. Otherwise, the land seemed empty.

'If you need a drink,' Inspector Singh called, 'hold the water in your mouth for as long as you can and then swallow it. That way, your body thinks it's had more than it really has. And the water lasts longer.'

It was a relief to enter the forest again. 'It almost feels cold!' Anji told her father, and felt happier.

'You remember Suresh and Hari?' Inspector Singh asked. 'The honey gatherers?'

Anji nodded. 'They used to come to the house with honey last year. But I've not seen them since I went to school in Amra,' she replied. 'It'll be nice to see them again.'

'Well, here's the track,' Inspector Singh said, moments later.

They walked on for a couple more minutes then came to a bend. Beyond it, Anji saw the two shacks. A dog was lying in the middle of the track between them and a radio was playing loudly.

Otherwise, there was no sign of anyone. Inspector Singh was just about to call a greeting, when a small girl on a red tricycle appeared, pedalling furiously.

She was heading for the dog. As they watched, she rang the bicycle bell and the dog sat up. Wearily, it sidestepped the child, looked up, saw the elephant and began barking hysterically.

Children appeared as if by magic. For a moment, they stood wide-eyed, then they surrounded the elephant in an excited, chattering crowd. Anji saw a woman's face peer out of a doorway. A man joined her.

'Hari!' called Inspector Singh, waving his hand. 'Are you well?'

Hari was better dressed than usual, Inspector Singh thought. He was wearing new trousers and a T-shirt. He looked almost prosperous. From the other shack, a woman came out to see what was causing all the excitement. She came to greet them, walking a little awkwardly, in high-heeled shoes. Anji stared in disbelief.

Inspector Singh recognised Suresh's wife immediately. She smiled up at him and that was another surprise. She was usually very sulky. He had never seen her smile before.

'Would you like some tea or some water?' she asked.

'Tea would be lovely,' he smiled back. 'Oh! And can the elephant have a banana or two, as well?'

She shouted at one of the children to go and pick some and the whole gang of them ran off to help.

'All dressed up and nowhere to go?' he teased.

She looked down and stooped to brush the dust off her shoes.

There was a gruff shout and she straightened up. Suresh emerged from the shack, scowling. 'Make the tea for our guests,' he shouted and said something to her as she went past. The radio was switched off.

Suresh came over and shook hands with Inspector Singh and then with Anji. He smiled up at them. 'What brings you here, Sahib?'

Inspector Singh told him about the tiger bones. 'I think someone's taken them and I'd like to know who.'

'If they were lying on the ground what harm

can there be?' Hari started to say when Suresh quickly interrupted.

'I've never seen these bones. Are you sure you looked in the right place?'

Inspector Singh nodded. 'Yes! They were there only last month. I saw them.'

Suresh spread his hands. 'This is news to us. I expect it was hyenas. We've had them around here as well. They killed a dog.'

Suresh's wife appeared barefoot and carrying a tray. On it were four small glasses of milky tea. The glasses were new and unchipped and had a pretty floral pattern on the outside. They drank in silence. The tea was hot and sweet and very refreshing. It was just what Anji needed. Inspector Singh handed back their glasses with a smile.

'The honey business must be booming!' he said.

Suresh nodded. 'It has been a good two months.'

Hari scratched his neck and said nothing.

'What about this big new tiger?' Inspector Singh demanded. 'Have you seen him?'

Suresh shook his head. 'We hear him roaring at night.'

'And I found his tracks,' Hari added.

'We can go one better in that case,' said Inspector Singh jovially. 'We saw him only about an hour or so ago. He's magnificent.'

'Where was this?' Suresh asked.

Hari shuffled his feet and looked away.

There was something almost furtive about his body language, Anji thought. Something not quite right. She prodded her father discreetly in the back.

But he did not seem to notice. 'By the stream,' he told them. 'They often rest up there. He was enjoying the shade.'

They left shortly after this. The children accompanied them along the track and stood waving goodbye when they plunged back into the trees.

'So the disappearance of the bones is still a mystery,' Inspector Singh said.

'Dad! Did you see the shoes she was wearing? The one who brought us the tea?'

The Inspector shook his head. 'No. Not particularly. That's Suresh's wife. She doesn't normally wear any.'

Anji groaned in disbelief. 'They cost a bomb! You wait till I tell Mum about them!'

Inspector Singh laughed. 'No! No! You've definitely got that wrong, Anji.'

'And I don't think you should have told them about the tiger,' she said, crossly.

Inspector Singh looked puzzled. 'Why on earth not?'

Anji shook her head impatiently. 'It's just a feeling, I've got.'

Inspector Singh laughed good-naturedly. 'That's my Anji!'

30

Over supper that evening, Anji related the events of the day.

'The tiger was absolutely huge!' she told Himal. 'Dad says it's the biggest he's seen in years! We were so close to him! It was magic!'

Himal looked envious but said nothing.

The Singh family was sitting together in the kitchen. Inspector Singh was reading a newspaper. Mrs Singh was sewing on shirt buttons and Himal and Anji were playing draughts. Anji's mind was not on the game. She kept looking at her father.

'Gotcha!' exclaimed Himal, taking her last three counters. He beamed at her in triumph. 'That's my game!'

'Dad!' Anji burst out, pushing the draughtboard away from her. 'Do you think the honey gatherers stole those bones?'

Inspector Singh looked up in surprise.

'Do you mean the old tiger bones?' Mrs Singh asked.

'Well, Dad!' Anji challenged. 'Do you?'

Inspector Singh shook his head. 'Perhaps it was the hyenas after all,' he said. 'I've known Hari and Suresh most of my life. They're the last people I'd suspect.'

Anji shook her head impatiently. 'But, Dad! Those shoes that woman was wearing!'

'Which woman? What shoes?' Mrs Singh demanded.

Inspector Singh folded his newspaper with a sigh.

'Mrs Suresh. The young one,' he told his wife. 'Anji is very suspicious because of the shoes she was wearing.'

'Mum! They must have cost thousands of rupees!' Anji interrupted. 'They were like the ones you tried on in the shoe shop. Remember what the salesman said? That the shoes were Italian inspired?'

Mrs Singh frowned then fixed her husband with a look. 'How can a woman like Mrs Suresh afford shoes like that? I couldn't think of buying them even on an Inspector's pay!'

'And did you see how smart Hari was looking?' Anji challenged. 'And the new toys the children had. And the radio?' She turned to her mother. 'They had a battery radio playing full blast.'

Everyone stared at Inspector Singh.

He became agitated. 'Yes! All right! They did look more prosperous. But Suresh told us they'd had a good couple of months. You heard him.'

'But, Dad!' Anji insisted. 'What about the shoes?'

'Perhaps she stole them,' put in Himal.

'And someone's definitely stolen those bones and I know who!' Anji stormed.

Inspector Singh put a hand to his head. 'Well,' he said slowly, 'even if they have, my real worry is who might have paid them the money to do it. So it can't just be Suresh and Hari, there has to be someone else involved, too.'

Himal's eyes gleamed. 'You mean like poachers? Or an organised gang?'

Inspector Singh nodded. 'That's my big worry.'

Mrs Singh bit off a length of cotton thread. 'You must tell the Superintendent,' she said. 'Why should you do all the worrying? He's in charge now. You give him the worry. How is he, by the way?'

Inspector Singh pulled a face. 'I haven't seen much of him. He's been travelling around the Park in that Range Rover of his. I don't think he likes elephants.'

Himal laughed. 'Someone told me that Dev's elephant, Daisi, tried to tread on his foot the first time he visited the stables.'

'What about his wife?' asked Mrs Singh.

Inspector Singh looked vague. 'She's still in Delhi,' he said. 'She's giving a very grand party next month. Apparently, the prime minister's going to be there. The Super's taking a week's leave for it.'

Mrs Singh digested this piece of news in silence.

Her husband looked at her. 'Do you know what I think?'

She shook her head.

'I don't believe he'll be here for that long. A year maybe. Not much more.'

'In that case, you must keep in with him,' she said firmly, and started to put her sewing things away. 'You need him to give you a good report. You're not too old for promotion.'

'But what about the bones!' Anji cried. 'What are you going to do about them?'

Inspector Singh put up a hand. 'Just wait, will you, Anji? I must think. Talk to Dev. This might just be a one-off situation. Or, there could be dreadful times coming again. I've got to get it right.'

'And don't forget to tell the Superintendent,' Mrs Singh said waspishly. 'It's his business, now.'

Anji looked at Himal and shook her head in despair. She thought of the tiger they had met that afternoon and her eyes felt suddenly hot.

'Don't spend too much time thinking, Dad, will you!' she said bitterly. 'If someone's already paid for those old bones, you know what they'll want next!'

And she left the room.

31

'Just a moment, Sir!' Inspector Singh called and hurried over to the Range Rover. He saluted smartly as the Superintendent stared out at him.

'Yes, Inspector? What is it?'

'Can I have a word with you, Sir?'

The Superintendent's fingers tapped the steering wheel. 'I'm just off,' he began, then grudgingly asked, 'What's it about?'

'A possible case of poaching.'

'What do you mean "possible"?' the Superintendent snapped.

Inspector Singh told him some of the events of the day before. When he had finished, the Superintendent scowled.

'Bones. Old bones! That had been lying there for six months!'

'Old bones today; new bones tomorrow,' Inspector Singh quipped.

The Superintendent looked at him blankly. 'Is this some sort of nursery rhyme, Inspector? Because if so, I really haven't got the time.'

'What I mean, Sir,' said Inspector Singh through gritted teeth, 'is that if someone's paying to have old bones taken out of the Park, you can be sure they won't stop there.'

'How do you know they're paying? It's probably scavengers. Wild dogs. That sort of thing. Look, Inspector, I'm more concerned about living tigers than a heap of old bones. And if you're so worried about them, it's a pity you didn't collect them, months ago! Now, I've got work to do.'

He started the engine. 'Oh! There is one thing,' he said. 'That end-of-term speech at the school, next week. I'll be doing it. I think they'd prefer to have the senior officer there. Don't you?' And he drove off.

'What am I to do, Dev?' Inspector Singh asked,

almost plaintively. 'He just won't or can't listen. Half the time I think he's laughing at me. He makes me feel stupid. I'm beginning to doubt my own judgement.'

Dev nodded in sympathy. 'He's like that with everyone. You're not alone. You should hear what Joshi says about him. Still,' Dev mused, 'Hari and Suresh, eh? Who'd have thought they'd get involved in something like this?'

'But we don't know that they are, Dev!' Inspector Singh cried. 'I'm most likely defaming them. I've only got Anji's word for any of it. These blasted shoes she keeps going on about. But I can't tell the Super that, can I?'

He began to pace up and down, clearly agitated. 'I can't tell him I'm suspicious of two hard-working men of otherwise blameless reputation, because of the unsupported imaginings of a twelve-year-old! Now can I? He'd sack me on the spot!'

Dev nodded. 'He would!' He clicked his tongue in sympathy and asked, 'So what do we do?'

'Keep a very close eye on the honey gatherers, for a start. Route patrols through their part of the forest. If they're guilty, it'll show them we're suspicious. And hopefully, none of this will ever happen again. It'd be a one-off incident.'

'And if they're innocent?'

'It'll be a warning to them to stay that way.' He thought for a moment. 'Ideally, I'd like to put out a secret patrol to watch them. One man and an elephant. Someone sensible.'

Dev nodded. 'I'll do that if you like. My ankle's fine now. But it'll be risky. We can't do it every night. They'd soon know we were there.'

Inspector Singh got up and looked out into the yard. A patrol was just coming in. He didn't recognise one of the mahouts. He looked about Himal's age.

'The vet was right,' he said gloomily. 'Remember that day with the wounded tiger? He said you know you're getting old when the mahouts start looking so young.'

Dev joined him. 'Well, he is young. Too young in my opinion. He's just arrived. Trouble is, like all these youngsters, he thinks he knows it all. He needs more training. A lot more.' He broke off. 'What's up? Hey! What's happening?'

Inspector Singh was dancing a little jig. His face was wreathed in smiles. He slapped Dev across the back.

'Watch it!' Dev cried, ducking away. 'What's got into you?'

Inspector Singh grinned at him. 'Dev, you're a genius! That's how we crack the problem. We'll set up a training camp in the forest. Reasonably close to the honey gatherers but not too close. By day, we can teach the new boys their business. Then, at night, we can keep an eye on things. It's brilliant!'

32

The school bus was packed that afternoon with happy, cheerful students. Tomorrow was the last day of term. Once that was over with, six weeks of glorious holiday stretched out ahead of them. The driver started the engine. It wheezed then grudgingly spluttered into life.

A boy was running for the bus, waving to the driver to wait. The driver saw him and deliberately started to pull out. There was a loud shout and a man fell off his bicycle. An ironic cheer went up from inside the bus. The driver looked out of his window, saw the man was unhurt and began to shout at him.

Yogi scrambled on board, panting hard. Himal

grinned and pointed to the seat he was keeping for him. The bus jolted forward as Yogi fell into it.

'He wasn't going to wait for you!' Himal exclaimed. 'He's a real pig! He reminds me of somebody.'

'How about Superintendent Malik?' Yogi suggested. 'My dad says he's a total swine.'

Himal nodded. 'I'm sure mine thinks the same.'

'Is that why he's talking to the school tomorrow and not your dad?' Yogi asked.

'He muscled in,' Himal said bitterly. 'My dad was really looking forward to it. But Malik pulled rank. He is a pig.'

'He's been giving my dad a hard time,' Yogi confided.

'He gives everyone a hard time,' Himal told him. 'Someone should teach him a lesson.'

'Like what?'

Himal shrugged. 'I don't know.'

'You talk big, Himal,' Yogi scoffed. 'But that's all you ever do.'

'Well you tell me, then,' Himal cried, stung by his friend's criticism.

'My dad says he's never been in a park like this before. He's a city boy.'

'He's a Delhi warrior,' said Himal. 'That's what my mum calls him. He doesn't even like elephants!'

Yogi looked at Himal. 'I bet he's terrified of snakes, then!'

'Wow! I bet he is!'

'Perhaps he should meet one?'

'Why not!' Himal laughed. 'Well, nothing too nasty. Nothing that's going to kill him or anything.'

A grin spread over Yogi's face. 'I've got just the thing!'

'What? A snake!'

Yogi chuckled. 'You know I've been doing a module on reptiles, this term? Well, I've got a rat snake in a box at home. I only caught it a couple of days ago. And now it's too late. We can use that.'

Hiaml's jaw dropped. 'You never told me!'

'Wasn't important.'

Himal grinned. 'It is now!'

'How about if I bring it to school tomorrow? Then when Malik gets up to talk, I slip out and let it loose in the back of his Range Rover?'

'You're serious!' Himal gasped.

Yogi nodded. 'On one condition. That you swear you'll not tell anyone!'

'I swear!' said Himal simply.

33

Suresh and Hari were cycling along the potholed road that led to Amra. Their bicycles were brand-new. The paintwork was immaculate and the handlebars glinted in the morning sun.

'Suresh,' said Hari, 'I am worried about Inspector Singh. Do you think he knows it was us who took the tiger bones?'

Suresh weaved his way around a particularly deep hole before replying. 'What does it matter? There's nothing he can do about it now. He has no proof. If he had, he would have been back the next day to throw us out of the Park.'

Hari did not reply. If anything, he seemed even more miserable. But as they reached the outskirts of Amra, he burst out, 'Suresh! This man Katni! Why does he demand to see us?'

Suresh stopped pedalling to let Hari catch up. 'How should I know?' he replied, with a shake of his head. They rode on together, ignoring the honking of an impatient car behind.

'Well, I don't like him. Or that Pauli creature.'

Suresh groaned. 'I am sick to death of you saying that, Hari. Especially when the only thing he's ever done to you is give you money.' He turned his head and spat at the overtaking car. 'You should be on your knees every night, thanking him,' he added, sarcastically.

Hari shook his head. 'But there must be a catch. All this money just for honey and some old bones?'

Suresh banged his fist down on the handlebars. 'Of course there's a catch,' he cried. 'Don't pretend to be so stupid. We work for him now. We do whatever he wants. That's what he's paying for!'

'That's because we know the forest,' Hari said. 'So what happens when he tells us he wants more. Forget collecting the peacock feathers and honey and pretty pebbles. Go for something else.

Something bigger. A tiger is what I'm thinking of.'

'Hari, you are a fool!' Suresh shouted. 'You are given a lot of money. Money for a new bike. Clothes for your wife and children. You take this money and spend it. Fine. But now you complain about a "catch"!' He looked at his friend in genuine astonishment. 'Your wife is happy. Your children are happy. So why can't you be?'

They waited at a railway-crossing while a goods train clanked past. They were in heavy traffic now. Hari leant towards him. 'I don't want to do it, Suresh. It's wrong. Killing.'

'Too late, my friend. You've spent their money.' There was contempt in Suresh's voice. 'Personally, a dead tiger means far more to me than a live one ever did.'

'You've changed, Suresh. You are so hard these days. You are not the man you used to be!'

Suresh swore violently. 'And you are so right, Hari! I am no longer a little nobody calling the likes of Dev Patel, 'Sir'. I'm a businessman now. I have a shirt and tie to wear whenever I want.' He thrust down hard on the pedals.

'You're a poacher,' Hari muttered, trying to

keep up with him. 'And I've been a fool. A greedy fool!'

They didn't talk for the next ten minutes while they cycled across Amra. When they got to the storehouse, Pauli himself opened the door. He took them along a short corridor, past boxes stuffed full of dried plants and scented tree bark, into a back room. They were surprised to find four other men there, squatting on the floor. Men like themselves. Men who avoided eye contact. No one spoke.

Katni came in. His manner was brisk and businesslike.

'You are wondering why I have called you here,' he told them. 'Now, I will tell you. We have been secretly visiting the tiger park for the past several weeks. And I can say with my hand on my heart, that it is wide open! There is no problem operating there as long as you are watchful and alert.'

He rubbed his hands together in mock excitement. 'The time has come for you to earn big money.'

One of the men squatting on the floor began to clap enthusiastically.

'I've even got you the latest steel traps!' Katni went on. 'Pauli and I will bring them round to you in the next few days. Then we'll show you exactly how to set them.' He paused for emphasis. 'Your job now is to find your local tiger trails and pick the best places for the trap.'

'Can we look at one now, please, Sir?' Suresh asked. 'Just a quick look.'

Katni considered. 'Sure. Why not?' He nodded to Pauli. 'Bring one out.'

There were a number of wooden crates standing along a wall, marked, 'Motorised Water Pumps'.

And below, in bright red paint, the words, 'Urgent – Government Property'.

Pauli raised the lid of the nearest one and began pulling out armfuls of packing material. He braced his legs and lifted out a trap by its closed, serrated jaws. Hari swallowed hard.

'Tell them about it!' Katni ordered.

Pauli looked down at the men. 'The base of the trap is fifty centimetres square . . .'

Hari listened in growing disbelief . . .

'You've got to force open the jaws and lay them

flat across the base,' Pauli told them. 'It'll take two of you to do it because the spring is so powerful.'

'We'll show you how to set the spring when we drop them off,' Katni added.

Pauli nodded. 'When the trap's set, you don't have to worry about some other animal, or even a man, setting it off. Only a tiger's heavy enough to do that. Nothing else can. Believe me.'

'And it only takes a tenth of a second for the jaws to mesh,' Katni told them with relish. 'No animal alive has got the reflexes to beat it. Not even a tiger!'

Pauli unwrapped a fresh wafer of chewing-gum. 'Once the tiger's caught, the only way it can get out is to bite its own leg off!'

He pointed to the heavy-duty chains at each corner of the base, and picked up a long spike.

'You'll need all four of these to stake it out. Make sure you bang the spike in all the way. Tigers are very strong,' he told them. 'You don't want a tiger dragging your trap away with it, do you? Because you'll be paying for it!'

Some of the men laughed.

'And don't forget to cover the plate and the

chains with grass or branches when you're finished.'

'We'll show you everything when we come out,' Katni told them, smoothly.

One of the men held up his hand. 'If we catch a tiger, what do we do then?' Several other heads nodded.

'Not "if" but when!' Katni corrected, with a forced smile. '*When* you catch it, get on your bike and ride like the wind to tell us. We'll do the rest.'

There was a murmur of excitement.

'What about our money?' someone else demanded. 'When do we get it?'

'In about two or three months' time,' Katni assured him. 'When the transaction is complete.'

There was a sharp intake of breath.

'Don't worry!' Katni reassured them. 'I'll pay you good wages each week as an advance. But you won't get the balance until the end. We don't want shopkeepers talking, do we? Or the police getting to know.'

The men murmured and looked disappointed.

'One last thing!' Katni called, and waited until they were looking at him again. 'Keep your mouth shut! Make sure your family does the same. If one word of this gets out and the authorities get wind of it, you'll be spending the next five years breaking rocks in Amra jail!'

The men nodded. He had a point. Their good humour returned and they filed out looking happy again. Only Hari did not join in the general enthusiasm.

34

Kuma and the cubs were hunting. Kuma was standing motionless, watching a grazing buffalo. The buffalo was by itself. The rest of the herd was forty metres away, standing around a small pool of water.

Behind her in the grass, the cubs were watching. They already knew a good deal about wild buffalo. A week ago, Taza had almost been gored by one. He had twisted away from the buffalo's long, curving horns in the nick of time. Soon after this, they found the body of a leopard that had been trampled to death by a herd. The cubs were now well aware of the danger.

As Kuma watched, the buffalo's head went

down and it started to graze. She studied the animal, carefully. It was in the prime of life. Its horns swept back over its head in a magnificent curl, two metres from tip to tip. It was the size of a large domestic bull.

During the next ten minutes, the tigers moved closer until there was only a thin screen of grass between them and the buffalo. The buffalo lifted its head. Kuma growled softly. Obediently, Phur stepped out into the open. The buffalo snorted and turned to face her. Phur walked towards it. The buffalo charged and Phur ran back into the grass. A white egret flew down and landed near the buffalo's back leg. Distracted, the buffalo shifted round and turned its back on the tigers.

Taza reached it in two leaps and jumped high over its rump, biting down into the backbone. The buffalo staggered, wheezing in shock, and stumbled. It went down on one knee. Taza's momentum carried him over its neck. As the tiger's feet touched the ground, he leapt away from the horns, doubled back and seized its hind leg. He bit down into the hock joint and wrenched with all his strength, trying to pull it over.

The buffalo bellowed in pain and staggered. Taza dropped the leg and clawed his way up its side. His claws dug deep into the buffalo's shoulders as he straddled the animal. The buffalo reared up and, like a flash, Kuma came out of cover in a crouching run and seized it by the throat.

Taza leant over and slid down its front leg using his weight as a tipping point. Together, the tigers hauled the buffalo over. As it crashed to the ground, they dodged the thrashing hooves. Crouching over the buffalo, Kuma found the windpipe. Whenever the buffalo tried to push back on to its feet, Kuma lifted her own hindquarters and maintained the killing pressure. Slowly, the buffalo's struggles weakened. Blood trickled from its nostrils. The great head lay motionless. The heart fluttered then died.

Kuma hung on for another two minutes after the final spasm. Then she dragged the body towards the long grass. She stopped only once to warn the rest of the herd to keep their distance. As the cubs watched, she licked the rump and settled herself down to eat. Soon, she was filled with a sense of complete well-being. The cubs paced up and down behind her and yowled with impatience.

35

Anji was in her room, reading. Himal was out somewhere with Yogi. The house was very quiet. Her mother was sitting out on the veranda writing a letter to her sister in Bangalore.

She heard the sound of her father's moped but decided to wait and finish the chapter. Soon, she heard him join her mother. Anji's window was directly above the verandah. She didn't mean to listen but she couldn't help overhearing.

Inspector Singh sat down with a groan and closed his eyes. 'That man Malik is so rude! I'm not sure I can take much more. I'm even beginning to dream about him.'

Mrs Singh licked the flap of the envelope and raised her eyebrows.

'I didn't tell you what happened the other day,' Inspector Singh went on.

'You mean the speech day nonsense,' Mrs Singh stated.

He shook his head. 'No! Something more important.'

'You're saying the school speech day is not important!'

Inspector Singh hurried on. 'You know he always wears shiny metal buttons on his uniform jacket?'

'So?'

'Well, he asked me why didn't I do the same? I told him that spitting cobras always aim at them. They think the buttons are eyes. And do you know what he said to me?'

She shook her head.

'Singh!' – he broke off here to explain – 'He always refers to me as "Singh". Singh, he says, you seem the sort of man who is afraid of his own shadow!'

Up in her room, Anji sat on the bed and gasped.

Unexpectedly, Mrs Singh took his hand. 'Listen, Dowi. Let me tell you what I think.'

Inspector Singh bent his head.

'Mr Malik is a very arrogant man. He is also a stupid man. He may, or he may not, know this. Probably he does not. But he must know his subordinates do not like him.'

Inspector Singh grimaced. 'You can say that again.'

'He's got his promotion because of his family connections and perhaps because no one wants him with them for very long.'

'You mean they kick him upstairs?'

Mrs Singh nodded. 'Perhaps. Now this is how I think you should treat him.' She ticked off the points on her fingers. 'Agree with him. Go along with his suggestions. Give him whatever he wants.' She became animated. 'I tell you now, if you do that, you'll be the first person to do so in a very long time. If he feels you are wanting to help him, maybe he'll start trusting you. Maybe!'

It was a long speech and Anji thought it a good one. She heard her father grunt but say nothing else. She got up quietly and went out. She met her mother who gave her a sharp glance.

'Anji! Please go and find your brother and tell him to come in. It's almost suppertime.'

36

The one thing Inspector Singh disliked doing above everything else was the Park accounts. He was not a natural bookkeeper. Columns of figures left him cold. He resented the time he had to spend getting the books to balance. He was poring over them now, trying not to use his fingers to count with.

'I hope none of your staff see you doing that,' Mrs Singh had told him. 'They'll think you a child. Why can't you use a calculator like everyone else?'

The doorknob rattled. He looked up crossly. He hated being disturbed when he was working like this. The Superintendent walked in. Inspector Singh politely rose from his chair. The

Superintendent waved him down and began to examine the photographs on the wall. He did so without a word. When he had finished, he stood looking out on to the roadway.

'You've got three windows, Singh. I've only got one. Why?'

Inspector Singh remembered his wife's advice and thought quickly. 'It makes the room very noisy, Sir! It's hard to concentrate. Too many distractions. But if you'd prefer it to your own, I'll move out now.'

Superintendent Malik said nothing. He remained where he was, gazing out.

'I'm not happy with the patrols,' he said slowly. 'That man Patel, for a start. He's scruffy and far too easy-going with the mahouts. They're more like circus performers than trained forest guards. I'm told he takes children out for rides. Your children.'

Inspector Singh gulped. 'He's an excellent man with elephants, Sir. There's nothing he doesn't know about them.'

But the Superintendent was not listening. 'And this man you've got in the stores. The fat chap.

What's his name? Josh? Joshi! Yes, him. I've found a lot of irregularities there.'

Inspector Singh took a deep breath and said gravely, 'You're absolutely right, Sir! We all need shaking up and I'm the first to admit it.' He stood up and addressed the Superintendent's back.

'What we need, Sir, is for you to order me to set up a training camp.'

Malik hesitated for a second. 'When did you last have one?'

Inspector Singh's heart lifted just a little. 'Not for some years. I'm afraid it takes an experienced officer like yourself to see when one is needed again.'

The Superintendent swung around. 'Yes. Of course! Just tell me how you see it being run, will you?'

He went and sat down in a nearby chair. 'On you go!' he ordered.

'Well, Sir,' Inspector Singh began, 'a training camp is your way of making sure every part of the organisation is able to carry out its role, efficiently.'

'And every part includes what?' Superintendent Malik asked.

'Everyone,' Inspector Singh told him. 'Elephants, mahouts, cooks, stores people, clerks and heads of departments. We test them all and if they're lacking in any way, we retrain them.'

The Superintendent nodded.

'We also check their personal standards. I know how keen you are on smartness.'

'A clean horse never came out of a dirty stable,' Malik agreed. 'And how long will all this take?'

Inspector Singh calculated. 'Two or three weeks. Or whenever you're satisfied. It's up to you.'

The Superintendent leant back in the chair. 'And just how is everyone involved?'

Inspector Singh pretended to look thoughtful.

'First of all, we need to find a suitable place to hold the camp. Then the stores people will have to organise the daily food and water for the elephants and ourselves. We'll need a cookhouse. Then there's tented accommodation for all personnel and the offices for your Headquarters staff. We still have to run the Park.'

'What about the training?' Malik asked.

'Let me give you just one example of what's entailed,' Inspector Singh suggested. 'Take the elephants. We've several newly joined mahouts. So let's see how good they are at controlling their elephants. Can they move backward in thick forest or in between thorn bushes? Can they rig a working harness? What do they know about foot rot or how to treat biting flies?'

The Superintendent looked impressed.

'Then there's the more advanced training,' Inspector Singh went on. 'What happens if a tiger attacks? What do they do? Or a snakebite on the tip of the trunk?'

There were footsteps outside. Dev Patel looked in. His cheery grin died away when he saw the back of the Superintendent's head. He put both fingers in his ears and waggled them.

Inspector Singh coughed quickly to hide a laugh.

'And the others? The cooks, the clerks and those wretches in the stores. What do we do with them?'

Inspector Singh considered. 'I'm sure you'd agree, Sir, that they'd all benefit from some army-style drill and cross-country runs. I know I would.'

The Superintendent's eyes gleamed. 'Absolutely! Very good. I like the sound of this.'

A thought struck him. 'Why can't we stay here and do it?'

Inspector Singh shook his head. 'It wouldn't be very real, would it, Sir! Too close to home comforts.'

'Of course! You're right,' the Superintendent agreed. 'Now how long is all this going to take?'

Inspector Singh pulled a sheet of paper towards him and picked up a pen.

'Let's say, a week to plan it. A day or two to get out there and set up the tents. Then two or three weeks' actual training.'

The Superintendent smiled!

'That's perfect,' he said. 'I'll be away in the middle of it. I'm in Delhi for a week. Maybe stay a bit longer.'

'Excellent! That'll give me time to get everyone smartened up for your final inspection.'

'And you can organise all this, Inspector?'

'With great pleasure, Sir.'

Superintendent Malik stood up. 'Very good, Singh! Very good indeed. It's a first-class idea.' He looked at his watch. 'I must be off.'

'Just one more thing, Sir,' Inspector Singh called

after him. 'Will it be all right for wives and children to visit the camp at weekends? It would be so good for everyone's morale.'

The Superintendent waved in acknowledgement. 'Why not!' he called.

37

Suresh's eyes gleamed. He gave a cry of triumph and pointed at the pugmarks in the sand.

'This is the place!' he cried. 'This is where the tiger comes to drink!' He stooped and expertly scanned the tracks. They belonged to a fully grown male tiger. He knew that by the sheer size of the pugs. They were as big as a child's head. It was certainly not the female with the two cubs whom he had often seen near here.

He sat on his heels and studied the approach route the tiger had taken. There were a couple of broken twigs hanging from a nearby bush. He examined them carefully and saw they had been freshly snapped. A bruised leaf lay on the ground, half buried from where the tiger had stepped on it. Further away, he found other pugmarks belonging to the same tiger but made earlier. They were full of loose dust.

He clicked his tongue in excitement. He had been right to choose this area. Tigers loved water. Even so, it had taken days to find a well-used tiger trail like this. He stood up and called Hari. 'This is the place! Now, we must fetch the trap.'

They took it in turns to carry it. They walked bent double, with the trap balanced across their shoulders. It was awkward and as heavy as a sack of maize. Their ribs and elbows were soon bruised and sweat was pouring off them by the time they got back.

Hari dropped the trap on the ground with an expression of loathing. He went to the stream and splashed water on his face and neck. Then slapped bad-temperedly at the flies. 'I do not want anything more to do with this,' he told Suresh. 'I shall hide in the forest from Katni and Pauli. They will never find me.'

Suresh looked at him, pityingly. 'But they know where your wife and children live. Why do you think everyone is as stupid as you?' He bent over the trap and heaved it upright. 'Stop talking so foolishly,' he gasped. 'Come and help me.'

They scooped sand away with their hands until the base of the trap fitted flush with the ground. Then they laid out the securing chains and drove the spikes deep into the ground. Carefully, they spread loose sand and twigs to hide it. Hari shivered. The back of his neck felt cold. He looked around.

'Now for the dangerous bit,' Suresh exclaimed. He put a hand on Hari's shoulders and shook him. 'I need your total attention,' he said. 'One mistake, any bit of not paying attention, and I will be dead.' He waited, watching the conflicting emotions chase across his friend's face. 'There's no going back now.'

'Why is it so quiet?' Hari asked. 'I feel we are being watched.' His eyes widened. 'It's the tiger! He's here. Creeping up on us!'

Suresh slapped him across the face. 'You talk like a silly girl!' he shouted. 'Now, do what I tell you!'

The slap seemed to calm Hari. He nodded at

Suresh. It took them some time to force the wicked-looking jaws down flat. There was just the faintest of clicks. Suresh gulped and wiped his hands on his T-shirt. 'Stand back! While I set the trigger,' he said hoarsely and waved Hari away.

He lay full length on the ground while he armed the trap. 'Now it is ready to strike,' he thought. He wiped an arm over his forehead and stared in fascination at the thing. It looked dead. There was no hint of the terrible power it contained. It was like a snake, rigid with ferocious energy. A split second's hesitation and the spring would release those gaping jaws with bone-cracking force.

'One more thing,' he told Hari. 'Go and find me a small branch with plenty of leaves on it.'

Hari watched him sweep the ground clear of any sign of their ever having been here. When he was satisfied, he tossed the branch away. He turned to Hari and laughed. 'Now all we have to do is wait! And dream how we'll spend all that money!'

38

Kuma was thirsty and feeling short-tempered. It had been a bad day for hunting. The langur monkeys had been particularly alert. Perhaps it was the flies that made them so active. They seemed to know exactly where to find her.

Six times, they had spotted Kuma stalking. They had seen her standing motionless in long grass; they had found her watching from thick cover and they had even discovered her hugging the shadows in the bamboo forest. Their warning screams had alerted the prey and sent it racing to safety. Her frustration had risen steadily all day.

Despite that, she had still launched four proper attacks although none of them had been successful.

The sambars and the chitals and the blackbuck had all dodged her outstretched claws and wrong-footed her. She had been outwitted every time and left to watch their flickering tails escape.

As darkness came on, she made her way towards the nearest water hole. The cubs followed, taking care to keep well behind. Kuma walked with her head low on her chest and her feet dragging. At one point she stopped and ripped her claws down the side of a tree. It made her feel a little better. But it did not last long. The irritations of the day soon returned. Her eyes and ears were full of dust. So was her nose. Her tongue was furred and her mouth was too dry to swallow comfortably.

The only thing she could think about was water. Cool, wet, delicious water. She wanted to run it through her mouth and wash out the dust deep in her throat. She remembered the sensation of dipping her head below the surface of the stream and the feel of it in her nostrils. And then some instinct brought her to an abrupt stop.

She held her breath and examined the sounds around her: the faint swish of wings as a hunting owl set off from its favourite branch; the excited squeaks of a pair of bush rats as they searched for grubs. She raised her head to catch the scents that were starting to rise into the cooler night air. And she found something that made her hackles rise!

It was no more than a fragment. If the evening breeze had not sprung up as she walked past, she would never have noticed it. Another tiger had brushed past the solitary grass stalk beside her. She hesitated. There was an old tree stump not far from here. It was one of her regular marking posts. It would be irresistible to any other tiger. But if she went there, she would be heading away from the stream. In a moment of indecision, she sat down and scratched. The cubs hesitated and did the same. Then she shook herself and walked towards the stump.

As she approached, she caught the scent again. It was still weak but by then she knew for certain that it was the big male tiger's. She snarled into the gathering night and went forward even more carefully. She stopped after every couple of metres and looked over her shoulder.

His scent was everywhere. It curled up to meet her and lay greasily on the fur along her sides. She licked at her chest and wrinkled her nose. She could even taste it. She called the cubs closer and walked on.

She examined the stump carefully and knew he had been there not long before sunset. He must still be near. She tried to remember all the places where he could lie in wait. And all the time, his smell grew stronger. And more threatening. She took a step backwards, then turned and ran.

By the time the moon rose, they were all tired and hungry. Kuma paced up and down in the deep shadow of a baobab tree and stared out at the cool brilliance. The big male might be anywhere. He could even be watching her now. There was a faint noise behind her. She whirled around. And at that moment, she heard the dreadful, grating roar.

The cubs ran and stood shivering beside her. There was another roar. And another. Terrible cries of agony and despair rolled over them. It was him! They all knew that. The forest was waking up. Its inhabitants listened in disbelief. Female monkeys clutched their babies tighter. Sleepy pigeons put their heads on one side and rolled their eyes in alarm. A family of hyenas stopped to listen then turned and trotted back the way they had come. A babble of confusion and delight swept through the treetops and across to the plains beyond. The great tiger was captured!

Kuma was running into the night towards the sound. The cubs were at her heels, desperate to keep up. Her mind was in turmoil. The screams she could hear unnerved her. But she had to see for herself. She had known great fear before. Stark terror, when the big male had attacked her. So what was happening now?

The roaring gave way to a loud sobbing. The sound filled her head. She flattened herself and crawled forward. She could smell the pungent stink of his urine. She could see him plainly out in the open between two bushes. He lay at right angles to the trap, held there by a front leg. The moonlight glinted on the cold steel that held him fast below the knee. He was sobbing and growling to himself. She heard the click-clicking of his teeth as they bit at the trap. A chain rattled and thumped on the ground.

As she watched, she saw him gather himself and

leap upwards. For a split second, she thought he had jumped clear. But the trap held him and he crashed to the ground. He gave a shriek. The hair on her face bristled. Her instinct was to rush out and help him kill the thing. But she was afraid.

He staggered upright. Kuma saw the trap was tilting to one side. He had pulled one of the securing stakes loose with that last despairing effort. She watched his head go down and moments later heard the sound of chewing. The big male was trying to bite through his own leg!

She heard something else. The high-pitched chatter of human voices. A sound that made her ears lie flat against her skull. It came nearer. There were two of them. Both of them men and very afraid. She could taste their fear. One carried a foul-smelling oil lamp. The flame inside licked in and out of the top.

Kuma measured the distance and knew that she could be at their throats in three strides. But before she could move, the big male sprang at them. The men screamed! The lamp sailed through the air and burst on the ground in front of her. There was a whoosh and there were flames everywhere.

Shocked, Kuma backed away. The flames crackled and darted towards her. Kuma fled.

Shar heard her go. He lay motionless across the trap. He waited for the men's screams to fade into the night then went back to his chewing.

39

A jet of flame roared into life underneath a row of metal containers. Sparks landed on a small patch of grass. It began to smoulder. Inspector Singh walked across and stamped on it. Earlier that morning, the cooks had dug an army cooker into the ground. They were now starting to brew tea for the midday meal.

Inspector Singh looked at his watch. They had been out here, setting up the training camp, for close to four hours. He was feeling reasonably pleased with progress. The only mishap so far had been caused by an elephant brushing past a wasps' nest. The elephant had bolted with its mahout. Dev was out there now, bringing them back. He had just reported progress on his mobile. Communications were working well, this morning.

The elephants were going back and forth bringing out everything needed to run the camp. Things like pressure lamps, canvas girth straps, kerosene and bags of rice. One more trip, Inspector Singh thought, should be enough. He wanted to have everything finished by early afternoon. After that, the elephants could rest under the trees, out of the sun.

The last of the tents were going up. He walked past and saw a sweating Joshi supervise the erection of his stores tent. It bulged and swayed drunkenly while the storemen argued where the tent poles should go. Others were banging in tent pegs and looping guy-ropes over them. As he watched, one of his own clerks came bustling past, carrying an armful of folders. His foot caught on a rope and he sprawled headlong. There was a good-natured cheer.

He went to inspect his own headquarters. A number of long wooden tables with heavy iron folding legs were stacked in a pile. A blackboard stood waiting outside the main tent, looking out of place. It was going to be used tomorrow to keep the scores for the team games.

He had spent a whole day choosing this place. It was half an hour in daylight from where the honey gatherers lived. At night, it would take at least twice as long to get there. It was a piece of luck, he thought, that the moon was full at present.

A thin trail of dust far out in the plain caught his eye. He studied it through binoculars. The Superintendent! The man was being almost friendly these days. Mrs Singh had been right. Malik was mellowing. He was certainly approachable. He had also made it clear that he wasn't going to be sleeping out here at night, which was music in the Inspector's ears. He and Dev were planning to leave the camp later that evening to pay a secret visit to the honey gatherers.

The dust cloud was growing closer. Inspector Singh walked over to the cookhouse. 'How long will the tea take?'

The senior cook took off the lid and peered in. 'Three minutes,' he said.

'The Super's coming. Just make sure the mugs are clean inside, will you!'

40

The men came at dawn. Katni was driving the four-wheel drive. Pauli sat beside him, holding a rifle between his knees. Suresh bumped around in the back. The wheel of his bicycle hung over the tailboard. It revolved slowly in the slipstream as the vehicle crashed and banged towards the trap.

They stopped ten metres away. Katni gave a low whistle. 'Jackpot!' He looked at Pauli and grinned.

Pauli grunted. He took a handful of bullets from his pocket and chose one. He slipped it into the breech and snapped the gun shut. 'Ready?' he asked.

Shar struggled to his feet. He snarled at the approaching men and tugged at his trapped leg.

The pain made him gasp. He staggered and almost fell. Sweat poured from him. He was weak and light-headed. He wanted to roar at these men and frighten them away. But his body refused to obey. He stood rooted to the spot, watching the ground going up and down.

Pauli lifted the rifle and squinted carefully through the sights.

'Side of the head,' Katni reminded him.

Pauli waited a moment longer then fired. The crack of the high-velocity bullet carried for three miles. Shar collapsed without a sound and slumped on to his side. As he did so, the forest erupted into another babble of confusion.

Screaming peacocks left the branches where they had been roosting. Flocks of parrots rose into the sky, protesting angrily. Whole families of monkeys swung through the trees, screeching and whooping in excitement. Herds of grazing deer lifted their muzzles and stood slack-jawed as the news reached them. The great tiger was dead. The men had killed him.

Pedalling furiously to join them, Hari heard it too and guessed what had happened. He caught up with the others just as Suresh and Pauli were forcing open the jaws of the trap.

'Grab his back legs!' Katni shouted at him.

It took the combined strength of all four of them to drag the tiger clear. 'He's a monster,' Pauli gasped.

Katni squatted down and ran his hand over the body. 'Nice shot!' he told Pauli. Then, looking up at Suresh, explained.

'Always shoot 'em in the side of the head. Customers don't like bullet holes between the eyes, any more. They say it's environmentally unfriendly or some such stuff.'

He burst out laughing. It was the longest speech Hari had ever heard him make.

Pauli chuckled. The compliment had pleased him. He walked to the vehicle and laid the rifle on the seat. He bent down and pulled out a roll of canvas. 'Skinning knives,' he told Hari. 'The best!'

Hari gasped. His face had gone grey. 'You are going to skin it?'

Pauli looked at him incredulously. 'Are you kidding!' 'Course I am. Tiger skins fetch good money.' He scowled. 'If you don't like it, don't look! Go and lift the trap. Drop it here. And then find a new place for next time!'

He watched Hari walk away then glared at Suresh. 'Don't tell me you're going soft as well?'

Suresh swallowed but he had himself well in hand. It was what he had been expecting. 'Not me,' he replied with a stern frown.

Pauli spat. 'Skinning a tiger's no problem,' he said. 'The legs can be tricky but once you've done them, the rest comes easy. Like peeling a banana. You've got to pull hard, mind.'

He unrolled the canvas holdall. Inside were six stainless steel knives lying in separate pockets. There was also a small cleaver. Pauli pulled out a knife with a short, serrated blade. He sat down with his back to the tiger's stomach and lifted up its front leg.

'You've got to cut it on the inside,' he told Suresh. 'So it won't show. Cut deep from the armpit down to the paw. Then grab both sides and tug.'

'Come on!' snapped Katni. 'We've not got all day.'

Pauli cut into the fur. He did the same with

the other legs. 'This one's a right mess,' he complained. 'Must have been chewing it. They do, sometimes.'

When he had finished, he picked up the cleaver, raised it above his head and chopped off the feet. 'Claws fetch good money,' he explained. 'I'll pull them out back at the shop.' He looked round. 'Where's the cooler box? Must be in the truck.' Then to Suresh, 'Get it, will you! It's that big blue freezer thing. You can't miss it.'

Pauli picked up a knife with a long curling blade. He thrust the tip under Shar's chin. 'Belly's next,' he told Suresh when he returned. 'All the way to his tail.'

When it was over, he rolled up the pelt and tied it with a piece of string. 'There's a sack somewhere,' he said. 'Find it, will you?'

Hari staggered past, the chains from the trap swinging round his ankles. He tried to look away but his eyes were drawn to the red, blotched thing lying on the ground. He gulped and was spectacularly sick.

Pauli's face wrinkled in disgust. 'Your mate's not got the stomach for this, has he?'

Suresh said nothing.

Katni came back from the four-wheel drive holding a chainsaw. He looked at Hari in disbelief and made a pointed detour around him. He yanked the starter and the saw burst into life. A small cloud of blue petrol fumes hung in the air. He throttled it back to a steady roar. 'Ready?' he called.

Pauli waved a hand then bent towards Suresh. 'The head comes off first. Put it in the cool box.'

'What do you want the head for?' called Suresh, beginning to feel queasy himself.

'Eyeballs, teeth. Whiskers,' Pauli told him. 'Big money. Next he does the legs. We don't bother much with the meat.' He prodded a bloody finger into Suresh's chest. 'Your job is to put the bones and other things into the cooler.'

Suresh made a face. Pauli saw it and laughed. 'You'll get used to it soon enough.'

An hour later, the three of them were bumping along a dried up watercourse on the way back to Amra. There was no sign of Hari. Suresh tried to remember when he had last seen him. He must have sloped off into the forest while they were cutting up the tiger. Hari was becoming a problem.

Pauli read his thoughts. 'Your friend didn't stay long, did he?'

Suresh shook his head.

Pauli tapped the side of the rifle with a stained finger. 'You make sure he does nothing stupid,' he said. 'Not unless he wants his own skin hanging on a wall. Or maybe his wife's!'

Then he smiled at Suresh. But there was no humour in his eyes.

41

'I don't like you rushing round like this so soon after lunch!' Mrs Singh complained.

'Mum!' protested Anji. 'We're meeting the elephants at two thirty. If we're not at the stables, they won't wait. You know what Dad said!'

'Well are you sure you've packed everything?' Mrs Singh demanded. 'Himal! Show me your toothbrush!'

'It's in my washbag!' Himal cried 'You saw me put it there!'

'It's in, Mum,' Anji assured her.

'And you'll make sure he changes his underclothes, won't you?' Mrs Singh told her daughter.

Himal stuck his fingers in his ears and ran down the verandah steps in fury.

'Oh, Mum!' groaned Anji. 'Leave him. Stop fussing.'

'Fussing? My two children are going to live in the middle of the wilderness and you call it fussing!'

Anji looked at her in disbelief. 'It's only for two nights, Mum. And Dad's going to be there and almost everyone we know.'

'And there will be scorpions and spiders and poisonous snakes living beside you.' Mrs Singh covered her face with her hands and moaned, 'Why did I let your father talk me into this?'

'Bye, Mum!' Himal shouted from the garden, wheeling out his bicycle.

Anji kissed her mother's forehead. Then, she too was shouldering a rucksack and mounting her bike. 'Bye, Mum!'

'We'll send you a postcard, if we're still alive!' Himal shouted.

'I thought she'd never let us go,' he told Anji as they entered the forest. 'What's wrong with her?'

Anji shook her head. 'It's just the way she is.

Anyway, we've still got lots of time to get to the stables.'

'I wonder how long it takes to get out there,' Himal said.

'Dad said about two hours,' Anji reminded him.

'Do you think Dev'll be there to meet us?'

'He'll be too busy testing the young mahouts,' Anji replied. 'That's what this training thing's all about.'

They rode in silence for a while and were not far from Park Headquarters when Anji, who was in front, gave a cry.

'What is it?' Himal asked as he caught up.

She pointed. A man's bicycle was lying in the ditch ahead of them. They stared at each other. They approached cautiously, pushing their own bikes in front of them.

The sound of retching stopped them. It was followed by a loud groan.

'Someone's being sick!' Anji hissed in disgust.

A man's foot appeared. There were more groans. He was lying under a bush. He looked up at them and hiccupped. His eyes were bloodshot.

'Hari!' cried Anji. 'What are you doing here!'

Himal gaped at her. 'You know him?'

'Of course I do. He's one of the honey gatherers. Mum used to buy lots from them last year. I saw them last week, when I was out there with Dad.'

Himal stared at Hari with interest. 'Well, he's as drunk as a skunk now,' he said. 'See!' He pointed to a half-empty rum bottle that lay on the ground near the man.

Anji came closer. The smell was disgusting 'Hari, what's happened? What's wrong? Can we help?'

Hari opened his mouth. A blob of vomit slid down his chin.

She looked at Himal. 'What's he doing here? He's miles from home.'

Hari's eyes flickered and he sat himself up. 'Inspector Singh,' he muttered. 'Bad . . . bad . . .' His voice was very slurred. He began coughing and they quickly moved out of the way. When the spasm was over, he reached out and unscrewed the bottle. The alcohol seemed to perk him up. He grinned and tried to focus on them.

'Tell Inspector . . . I'm sorry . . . so sorry . . .'

'Sorry about what?' Himal demanded.

Anji knelt down beside him. She picked up one of his hands. It was as cold and as bony as a bird's claw.

'Tell us, Hari. We'll help you. I promise.'

Hari nodded and dribbled for a while. Then, 'Tiger . . . big tiger . . . bones . . .'

Himal squatted down beside his sister. 'This was no joke,' he thought. The man really did have something to tell.

'Have you killed a tiger!' he demanded.

Anji caught her breath. 'Himal!' she gasped.

Hari's eyes closed. His body began to rock backwards and forwards. 'Yes . . .' he said, eventually.

'Where?' Himal asked.

But Hari did not seem to have heard.

Anji rubbed the back of his hand. 'Don't worry,' she told him. 'We'll tell Inspector Singh. I'm sure it wasn't your fault.'

Hari made a horrible cackling noise. It took them some time to realise he was laughing. 'I . . . dead man too . . .'

Himal spoke very deliberately. 'Where did you kill the tiger, Hari?'

But Hari did not reply. He hummed a snatch of tune instead.

'Where's the tiger, Hari. Please tell us.'

'Two tigers . . . one dead . . . one soon dead . . .' Hari wheezed.

'Where!' Himal shouted.

'Same place . . . bones . . . more bones . . .' and he fell asleep in front of them.

'He's sitting upright,' Himal said. 'So he won't choke on his own sick. I don't see what else we can do. Come on! Or we're going to be late.'

42

'He said what!' Inspector Singh demanded.

Himal turned to his sister. 'Bones. Lots more bones. Didn't he, Anji? That's what he told us.'

She nodded. 'And he said there were two tigers.'

'One dead and another one dead,' Himal added.

'Soon to be dead,' she corrected.

Dev stood up and began to pace up and down inside the tent. The light from the pressure lamp threw his shadow across the canvas. Outside, the sun had just set and night was already crowding in on the neat rows of tents.

'Let's just get this straight so that even I can understand,' Dev insisted. 'Hari mentioned two tigers. One dead and the other . . .'

'Soon to be dead,' Anji confirmed.

'You know what this tells me?' Inspector Singh looked round at them. 'There's a trap already set, waiting for the next tiger to come along.'

'Why did he say he was a dead man?' Himal asked.

Dev drew a finger across his throat. 'The other poachers. Who else?'

'Let's just talk about tigers, shall we?' Inspector Singh said, impatiently. 'There's a trap out there. Possibly in the same place or close to wherever the first one was.'

'How do you know that?' Anji queried.

His father shook his head. 'I don't. I'm just trying to make an informed guess. The first trap's been well sited. Probably, some good tracks there. It's been successful. It's also heavy to move around. So why not leave it where it is? That's how I see it. Agreed?'

They nodded.

'So we've got to work out where that could be.' He looked thoughtful. 'Hari mentioned "bones" a lot, didn't he?'

'I thought he meant the dead tigers,' Himal

said. 'Lots of their bones. Isn't that what the poachers are after?'

'What about those bones that went missing?' Dev asked. 'The old bones we couldn't find?'

Inspector Singh nodded. 'The ones we think Suresh and Hari took.'

'To buy Mrs Suresh's shoes!' Anji cried in triumph. 'I told you! Didn't I!'

'And Hari's new bike!' Himal exclaimed. 'I bet Suresh's got one too!'

'Do we arrest them?' Dev asked, looking at the Inspector.

'Not right now. That would be a mistake.'

'Why?' Anji cried, frowning.

'What happens if they won't say anything?' asked Himal.

'That's exactly it!' Inspector Singh agreed. 'If we pick 'em up, we'll warn off the whole gang. We've got to get the top men not just the little guys at the bottom.'

'Otherwise, it'll start up all over again in a few weeks,' Dev agreed.

There was a silence while they thought about this.

'So where is this damn trap, then?' Dev said, crossly.

'Bones!' said Inspector Singh, thoughtfully.

'And tiger tracks!' Anji interrupted. 'Dad!' she cried. 'Remember that huge tiger we saw? And his tracks?' Her voice trembled. 'That was near the place where you said the old bones were. Hari's bones!'

'The big flat rock!' Dev shouted. 'That's it!'

'My God! You're right!' Inspector Singh roared. 'Anji! You're a genius!' And he hugged her. 'It may be totally the wrong place,' he warned, a few moments later. 'But it's the best guess I can think of. Well done!'

'That's why we didn't hear anything last night,' Dev told him. 'We were waiting out on the other side.'

'And that's a long way from the flat rock,' Inspector Singh nodded.

Anji grabbed her father's arm. 'If we go there now, we can scare off any tigers and find the trap tomorrow. Then we can get rid of it!'

Himal punched the air. 'Brilliant!'

Dev and Inspector Singh looked at them and

said nothing. Slowly, Dev shook his head.

'What's the matter?' Anji demanded. 'Why are you looking like that?'

'It doesn't work that way, Anji,' Dev told her. 'I'm sorry.'

Anji stepped back in confusion. 'I don't understand! What's wrong? Why can't we do it now?'

'Oh God!' Inspector Singh moaned.

Anji and Himal stared at him in disbelief.

He took a deep breath and faced his children.

'Because, Anji, we need to catch the gang red-handed. To do that, we need a tiger in that trap.'

She stared at him in horror. 'You want another tiger killed!' Tears welled up. She brushed them away. 'You can't mean that! It's crazy! You're supposed to be the good guys. But you're not, are you? You're as bad as them!'

And she stumbled out into the night.

43

Dev found her an hour later in the elephant lines. She was standing with her arms around Daisi's trunk.

'You shouldn't be here,' he told her gently. 'This is all new for them. You could easily not be recognised and get bumped into, or something.'

He took her unresisting hand and brought her away. The moon had not yet appeared but the starlight was bright enough for them to find their way out of the trees unaided.

Anji stared up at the countless other worlds that wheeled and swung their way through the heavens towards eternity. As she did so, some lines from a

poem they had learnt at school flashed through
her mind.

> '*Did he smile his work to see?*
> *Did he who made the Lamb make thee?*
> *Tiger! Tiger! burning bright*
> *In the forests of the night*'

'What's Dad doing?' she whispered.

'Your father's already left,' he told her. 'He's got
a good mahout with him. They're heading for the
flat rock. They'll wait there till dawn. If the
poachers come, he'll call us. We're taking it in
turns. I'm out there tomorrow night.'

'And what do you do if anything happens?'
she asked.

'I bring out the rest of the mahouts and we'll try
and cordon off the area.'

'And arrest the poachers when they get there?'

'Yes!' Dev nodded. 'That's about it.'

'And what happens to the tiger?' she asked.
'Won't it be roaring in pain and trying to get
free?'

The moon was rising quickly. It was already

above the horizon. He could see her face quite clearly.

'Anji, listen!' He hesitated. Then said, 'How long have we known each other?'

She turned her head away.

'All your life,' he answered for her. 'Have I ever let you down? Told you a lie? Put a scorpion in your hand instead of a sweet?' He waited but there was no response. 'If we just go and get rid of this trap, supposing we ever find it, then don't you think the poachers will just set another one? Somewhere else? Perhaps miles away?'

She frowned.

'If we do it your way, there won't be just one tiger in trouble, there'll be all the other ones the poachers go on catching. But if we do it our way, then yes! There will be a tiger in agony but we'll also have the poachers behind bars. Now which is it to be?'

Anji wrapped her arms around herself and said nothing.

Dev sighed. 'I'd better call your father and tell him you're all right. He's sick with worry about everything.'

She followed him. When they reached the headquarters' tent, she cried out, 'Dev! I want to be there tomorrow night! Hari told us! Himal and me. It's the least you and Dad can do. Promise you'll take both of us out there!'

44

Dev peered at the luminous dial of his watch.

'What's the time?' Anji whispered.

'Five minutes to midnight,' he muttered. 'Almost time to call your father.'

She was surprised how cold it was out here. And frightening too. Moonlight streamed through the trees in shafts of eerie blue light. It dappled the ground in front of them with pockets of deep shadow.

Owls were hunting and the air was full of squeaks and sudden cries. There were rustlings in the branches above them. Anji did her best not to let her imagination get the better of her. Not far away, she could make out the dark bulk of another elephant. The mahout was called Ali and he had Himal with him.

The two elephants were about a hundred metres from the flat rock. They had already been waiting there for four hours. It would be dawn in three more. Daisi's stomach began to rumble. To Himal, it sounded like the distant roll of thunder. It easily drowned Dev's voice as he called Inspector Singh, who was forty minutes away, back at the training camp.

Himal remembered his father's words to Dev earlier that evening.

'Remember what soldiers say about war, Dev? That it's five per cent action and the rest plain boredom? So let Himal and Anji try it for themselves. They won't come to any harm!'

'Dad was spot on,' thought Himal. He was stiff and cold and all he wanted to do was sleep. He tried blinking rapidly to wake himself up. But it had no effect. His eyelids were growing heavier and heavier. He had a sudden vision of the camp bed waiting for him. Then he remembered his far more comfortable bed at home. And that made it worse. His head drooped.

There was a terrible roar. His elephant screamed and began backing away. Ali clapped his feet hard behind its ears, and broke into a torrent of words. Himal hung on. There was another roar and the hairs on his arms began to bristle. He heard Anji cry out and Dev's voice, suddenly loud.

'Calling, calling base. We have contact. Tiger! Tiger! Over!'

The tiger was roaring continuously. Its agony too dreadful to listen to. He had never imagined there could be so much pain. Himal shivered violently and felt suddenly very scared.

45

Hari came to, slowly. He was sitting on the ground with his back against something hard. His head ached abominably and his mouth was like sandpaper. His body ached all over. He wondered where he was but made no attempt to move. He could hear the whine of insects and a nightjar was croaking nearby. He opened one eye. And then the other. He lay there unmoving, absorbing familiar sounds.

As his eyes adjusted to the grey light, he saw he was surrounded by trees. Tall trees. There was something familiar about them. It took him a little while longer before he grunted in pleasure. He was back in his own part of the forest.

He had no idea how he got here. No memory at all. He vaguely remembered cycling. That must be why the tops of his legs were so sore. Some time later still, he decided he wanted to go home. He heaved himself up, clung to his tree and took several deep breaths. After a bit, he felt better.

But he was so thirsty! His tongue kept sticking to the roof of his mouth. Water! That's what he must find. And he could remember now where the stream was. He was congratulating himself, when the agonised moan of a tiger changed everything. He stood transfixed, listening in disbelief. Memory returned in a flash and dragged him back to reality. He was no longer Hari the honey gatherer, the forest dweller. Friend to all creatures. He was instead the great betrayer. The eternal human exploiter.

He stood in the middle of the glade, thrust his arms towards the dawn and begged for forgiveness. He had done this! He was responsible. Fingers of sunlight touched the clouds far above his head. Some inner voice told him to run towards the tiger. He had no plan. No idea what he could do to help the animal. But every instinct told him he must go there, prostrate himself and beg for pardon.

He ran, stumbling along, sometimes calling out for mercy but most of the time just sobbing. The trees were becoming smaller. Soon, they gave way to bamboo forest. There was a low mound right in front of him made of sticks and pieces of bamboo. He was drawn towards it and lengthened his stride so he could jump over it. As he leapt, he saw there were a number of large white eggs lying at its centre.

His brain told him what this meant in the split second before his feet landed on the far side. He stumbled and looked into the eyes of the striking king cobra. He felt its fangs thud into his shoulder. He heard it growling, felt the venom burning deep inside his skin, and saw its hood inflate still further. The second bite pierced the inside of the arm he flung up to protect his face. He screamed as the side of the cobra's hood brushed his cheek.

Then he was blundering past, running like a dead man on stiffening legs. Running into oblivion. No longer thirsty.

46

Pauli was singing and beating time on the side of the four-wheel drive. Suresh did not know what the song was but he tapped his foot all the same. He had been lucky and he knew it. He had told the men that Hari had fallen and sprained his wrist. They seemed to believe it. They hadn't mentioned Hari since. Suresh grinned in relief. He'd sort Hari out, later.

He drew out a tin of cheroots. They were the very first cheroots he had ever bought. He hesitated then offered them to both men in front. It was something he had never done before and he braced himself for their refusal. But to his delight, they each took one. A glow of pride spread through him. He was accepted! He sat back and thought how lucky he was.

Pauli was thinking along the same lines. A cheque for one hundred thousand rupees had recently been paid into his bank account. And like Suresh, he knew there was a lot more to come. He glanced across at Katni. The manager would be getting a lot more, of course. But he didn't resent it. Katni was the boss after all. Besides, Pauli's needs were simple. He already had enough money to retire. He went on banging his hand on the door and wondered about the tiger waiting for them in the trap.

Katni swore and came to a stop. Ahead of them, the trail forked. 'Which way?' he demanded. 'I've forgotten.'

Suresh leant over and indicated. 'Not far now,' he told them.

'Listen!' cried Pauli. 'I can hear it'

'Through there.' Suresh pointed. 'The trap is on the other side of those trees.'

Katni made a wide sweep then braked when he saw the tiger. They stared at it.

'Young female, I'd say,' Pauli said, sounding disappointed.

'OK. Let's get on with it!' Katni ordered, switching 'the engine' off.

Suresh barked his shins on his bicycle pedal as he climbed out. Pauli was already squinting down the rifle sights. There was one last snarl of defiance from the tiger. Then came the crack of the gun and Phur slumped down.

Suresh thought he heard an elephant trumpeting. But it was hard to tell with all the other noise. There it was again! Funny things, elephants, he thought. The smell of blood always upset them. It made them unpredictable. Should he warn the others? Pauli had put the rifle back on the seat and was already sorting out his knives.

Suresh bent down instead and dragged out the big cooler box. He went to join Pauli by the trap.

'Not much more than a big cub,' Pauli grumbled as Suresh squatted beside him.

Suresh looked at the tiger that had once been Phur. He reached out and stroked its side. They were beautiful creatures, after all.

Pauli brought the cleaver down hard. The paw flopped to one side. He did it again and severed it. 'In the box!' he grunted, handing it to Suresh.

As Pauli began to skin the carcass, Suresh hesitated. The elephants were still there. Nearer if anything. A lot nearer. He got up and stared around. Katni was approaching with his chainsaw. Suresh walked away. He did not like to watch this part.

Was that something moving? Something a little way inside the trees? Suresh stared in disbelief. There were two elephants there. With people on them! He turned to shout a warning. There was a loud roar as Katni started the saw. Open-mouthed, Suresh looked back. He could see Dev Patel. With a child behind him! Suresh panicked and ran.

'He's seen us!' Himal cried.

'Wait for it!' Dev shouted. He grabbed his whistle and blew two long blasts.

Anji saw the man with the chainsaw bend over the tiger and screamed.

Now Pauli was looking around. Suresh! Where the hell was he going?

Katni throttled back on the chainsaw and rolled the tiger's head to one side with his boot. He looked at Pauli. The man's mouth was wide open.

He was pointing at something. Katni spun round and his world turned upside down!

Elephants were crashing out through the trees. A great ragged line of them, trunks held high over their heads, trumpeting and screaming. Huge wrinkled legs rising and falling and pounding the ground. Their mahouts bent low, urging them on towards the men, encircling them. In the middle of the line was Inspector Singh, yelling like a madman.

It was getting difficult to see the trap. There was dust everywhere. Thick clouds of it, rising higher all the time. The elephants surged in and out like blurred shadows.

'Look! He's getting away!' screamed Anji.

They had a brief glimpse of a man running and ducking through all the confusion. Then he was past the elephants, out in the open, racing for the four-wheel drive.

'The rifle's in there!' Himal shouted a warning.

Dev was turning Daisi round, shouting at the top of his voice. A cloud of dust rolled over them. Blinding them all. A large grey shape loomed up in front. Dev screamed a warning but it was too late.

The elephants collided with a bone-jarring thud. Daisi's legs stuck out in front of her. Earth sprayed up as she ploughed two great furrows through the ground. She came to a stop and rocked over on one side. Himal leapt clear, landed safely and saw the outline of the four-wheel drive ahead.

He ran towards it and realised he was not alone. The man was running towards it, coming in from the side. Himal thought he had a knife in his belt but couldn't be sure. There was a roaring in Himal's ears. The ground was shaking all around him. He knew he wasn't going to get there in time. The man was reaching for the door.

An elephant thundered past. Himal leapt to one side. He heard Anji's voice screaming from somewhere high above him. The man had the rifle. It was at his shoulder. Then a long, grey trunk came swinging down and knocked him over.

The man was trying to get up. The rifle lay on the ground only a metre away. Himal bent and seized it. And fell. He heard the man cursing. Felt a hand grab his ankle. Now there were elephants coming in from all sides. And shouting and more dust. Someone bent over him and pulled him to his feet. He saw his father's face. There were tears running down his cheeks. Himal heard his name shouted. His father turned and reached out towards Anji. Then they were all hugging each other and nothing else seemed to matter.

Postscript

Both Pauli and Katni were arrested on the spot by Inspector Singh and taken to Amra. They are in prison there serving an eight-year sentence. Suresh hid in the forest for two days then went to Park Headquarters and gave himself up. He was given five years in gaol.

No one ever found Hari's body. It was almost certainly eaten by scavengers. Or perhaps a tiger came across it. Poor Hari. He really made a mess of everything. His spirit is probably still wandering somewhere in the forest.

Mr Sam disappeared without trace. But it is a certainty, that someone very like him will be visiting any one of a hundred towns similar to Amra in the next few weeks, to set up another poaching network. Sadly, because of rural poverty and the ever increasing demand for tiger products, many more poor people will be sucked into this disgusting trade.

The Superintendent left Kanla Tiger Park soon after the events described in this book. He received much praise for the actions of his staff and took up an important post back in Delhi. He unbent sufficiently at the end to tell Inspector Singh that he had recommended him for promotion. On the day he left, he confided that, if there had been one single event that made him want to return to Delhi, it was finding a large black snake loose in his Range Rover!

Dev and Inspector Singh were both promoted. They are still at Kanla and, between them, run the Park very well. To date, there have been no more poaching attacks there. But as Dev always says, 'We all know it's only a matter of time.'

Mrs Singh is rightly proud of her family and as the wife of a Chief Inspector, she now plays a prominent part in the Amra social scene. She still dispenses good advice and impossible demands in equal measure.

Anji and Himal are still at school but starting to think seriously about their futures. After all that has happened, Himal is more determined than ever to go on fighting for the survival of tigers. He is torn between following in his father's footsteps or going to university and then working for a wildlife charity.

Anji was devastated when she saw Phur's body in the trap. She spent many months brooding about it. More recently, she has decided to combine her love of animals with a desire to give them practical help. She has decided to become a vet.

And the tigers? There has been no sign of Taza but this is not surprising. The life of a male tiger is lonely, often short and always precarious. We hope he has managed to survive. Kuma, however, has been very successful. She has raised three more cubs who all survived to adulthood. The female cub now has territory bordering on her mother's. Kuma is expecting another litter in the next few weeks. She has been busy looking for a new nursery. Her mate is an even-tempered six-year-old.

Kuma will sometimes go to the flat rock and stand there. It is a secret place of hers. Perhaps the spirits of Poga and Phur are still there? After all, their blood has watered the grass and the new trees that have sprung up. We will never know.

We wish her and all her kind the very best of good fortune. But sadly, so long as humans kill tigers, their survival has to remain doubtful. May Everyone's God Be With Them!

WHY I WROTE THIS BOOK . . .

Four years ago, I read a newspaper report that poachers had broken into a zoo in Hyderabad, southern India, killed a tiger, skinned it and then cut it up into body parts. At first, I was so angry I could hardly believe it. Why would anyone want to do that? Then, I began to do some research and what I found made me write this book.

The tiger is now all but extinct in China, Siberia and South East Asia. It could vanish from India itself in the next few years. You will be the last people to have any chance of seeing a Bengal tiger in the wild. As things stand, by the time you leave school, the only tigers left will be those in captivity.

A hundred years ago there were about 100,000 tigers in India. Today, there are thought to be less than 2,000. So what's caused this?

Poaching is by far the biggest threat to the tiger. Tigers across the whole of India are trapped and killed so that their bones, claws, whiskers, livers and other body parts can be smuggled into China and used to make Traditional Medicine products.

A single tiger carcass will be worth £30,000 by the time it reaches these manufacturers.

Fighting poachers is an expensive business and for many years India has been unable to spend the money needed. The Park wardens who patrol the tiger reserves are often poorly equipped, unarmed, understaffed and badly paid. Yet they are the front line against today's well organized poaching gangs. In *Tiger!* Inspector Singh and his team patrol the tiger park on elephants. They're lucky! Many real life wardens have only got bicycles!

There is also a huge and growing problem as India's population continues to grow. People need space. They need food. In rural areas, this means they will clear scrub and cut down trees so that they can grow crops. The trouble is the tiger needs this space as well.

A fully-grown tiger will eat on average fifty prey animals a year. For a tigress raising cubs, this can be as high as seventy animals. However, humans and domestic animals soon drive away the tiger's natural prey. And when this happens, the ground is lost to the tiger for ever. Ironically, India's current economic boom is destroying even more natural habitat as roads, dams and powerlines are built. Many more thousands of square kilometers of grassland and forest are being lost each year because of industrialisation.

Tourism can also make local people resent tiger conservation. Some of India's poorest people live on the tiger reserves. They live in shacks with no running water or electric lights. Meanwhile, tourists staying in nearby modern hotels pay hundreds of pounds a night hoping to see tigers. Sadly, very little of this money reaches the local people, who become angry and hostile towards tiger conservation. In some places, poachers have been able to move into these reserves and now operate freely there.

This is a very brief overview of some of the problems facing the Bengal tiger. The good news is that the Indian Government has now stated its determination to fight the poachers and to clamp down on their operations. It has set up the 'Tiger Taskforce', chaired by the prime minister to consider ways of saving the tiger from extinction. We can only hope that they will be in time.

POACHING

People poach tigers to make money. There are close to 800 million people in India who live on less than £1.50 a day. To some of them, poaching seems the only way of earning desperately needed money. They will be paid between £10–20 for a tiger carcass. While this is peanuts compared to the £30,000 the dead tiger will eventually be worth, it is still a great deal of money to them and their families.

These people make up the bottom rank of poachers. While others set up local networks, bribe officials or smuggle the carcass out of India, their job is to find the tiger trails and set the traps. In *Tiger!* the honey gatherers, Suresh and Hari, are typical examples of such 'foot soldiers'.

Suresh and Hari were supplied by the gang with heavy-duty, steel traps. These traps need at least two men to force the heavy, serrated jaws apart. The jaws are held wide open by a powerful spring. Only the weight of an animal as big as a tiger will set off the trap. When this happens, the jaws mesh together with lightning speed and catch the tiger at the knee joint. The tiger can then only escape by chewing through its own leg. The animal is later shot by the poachers.

Poachers will also poison the bodies of dead cows or water buffalo. During hot dry summers, forest pools and small watering holes are also often poisoned.

Tigers are also electrocuted. Poachers will attach wires to overhead power lines and then lay them across game trails used by tigers.

Tiger poaching is a well-organised and highly profitable business. It is controlled by wealthy criminals operating out of the major cities. They are believed to have politicians, senior officials, police and customs officers on their payrolls. They deal directly with the Traditional Medicine manufacturers in China and they are responsible for getting dead tigers, out of India.

TRADITIONAL CHINESE MEDICINE

This is the root of the problem. And it is the reason why the Bengal tiger will almost certainly be extinct in the next five years, unless some sort of miracle occurs.

For the last 1000 years, Chinese culture has believed the tiger has mystical medicinal powers. Today, almost one quarter of the world's population will at one time or another consider using a tiger product as legitimate health care.

Tiger claws, teeth, bones, eyeballs, whiskers, tail, blood and dung, are all used to make traditional Chinese medicines. In fact, every part of the tiger is used. Tiger teeth are used to treat fever; tiger eyeballs help cure malaria and epilepsy. Whiskers are used to treat toothache. Tiger dung cures boils and alcoholism.

Bones are especially important. Small slivers are sliced off and ground into powder for the patient. Tiger products can also be bought as factory-made pills, powders and tonics.

While China, Japan, Thailand, Korea and Taiwan are the largest consumers of Traditional Medicine there are many thousands of shops and other outlets in the USA, the UK and Australia.

The worldwide market for tiger products is now

worth 3 billion pounds a year. And the demand is increasing. In the past year, for example, there has been a sudden upsurge in demand for tiger skins which are worn as fashion statements by wealthy Tibetans and Chinese at horse fairs.

The outlook for the tiger is very grim.

SO WHAT CAN YOU DO?

At first sight, not very much. But public pressure – at home and internationally – can make a difference. Young people have a right to know what is happening in the world they will soon be going out into. The deliberate slaughter of a species as magnificent as the tiger must be fought with every legitimate weapon.

To find out more visit:

Wildlife Protection Society of India –
http://www.wpsi-india.org

Tigers in Crisis –
http://www.tigersincrisis.com

Save the Tiger Fund –
http://savethetigerfund.org

World Wildlife Fund –
http://www.worldwildlife.org